CAVEMAN LOVE

Busy
Let
Sin

Cherie Denis

EROTIC ROMANCE

Siren Publishing, Inc.
www.SirenPublishing.com

A SIREN PUBLISHING BOOK
IMPRINT: Erotic Romance

CAVEMAN LOVE
Busy
Let
Sin
Copyright © 2011 by Cherie Denis

ISBN-10: 1-61034-254-2
ISBN-13: 978-1-61034-254-4

First Printing: January 2011

Cover design by Jinger Heaston
All cover art and logo copyright © 2011 by Siren Publishing, Inc.

ALL RIGHTS RESERVED: This literary work may not be reproduced or transmitted in any form or by any means, including electronic or photographic reproduction, in whole or in part, without express written permission.

All characters and events in this book are fictitious. Any resemblance to actual persons living or dead is strictly coincidental.

Printed in the U.S.A.

PUBLISHER
Siren Publishing, Inc.
www.SirenPublishing.com

DEDICATIONS

Busy

I want to give special thanks and love to my Mom who, along with my husband, encouraged me to follow my dream.
Thank you, Mom for all your hard work on my promotional material. I'd have never gotten it all done without your help.

Let

This is dedicated to the one I love. My own caveman, my lover, my friend. Thank you, sweet man, for your encouragement and love.

Sin

This book is dedicated to my editors.
I've taken 4 classes in punctuation and got As in all 4 classes, but without my editors I'd still be in punctuation hell.
Thank you all so much.
Cherie

SIREN PUBLISHING *Allure*

BUSY

CHERIE DENIS

Caveman Love

BUSY

Caveman Love 1

CHERIE DENIS
Copyright © 2011

Gem sighed when she spotted her father, Tog, stomping through the cave opening. She turned to check the fire. He stood behind her, and she shivered. He had brought the cold air with him along with his usual frown. Why did he never smile? He was always so angry.

She pushed her hair off her face and stared into the fire. She knew better than to look into his eyes and welcome him home. He would smack her for being rude. Women did not look into a man's face unless it was the face of their mate. Women who made eye contact with a man, even one's father, were considered aggressive and unmanageable. Gem's father's hand was very hard. She should know. He had used it many times on her before she learned to be subservient.

"Uh," he grunted.

She signed her greeting.

She knew what his next question would be and waited silently for him to sign his wants.

His fingers flew. "Is my meal ready, girl?"

"Yes, Father. It is ready," she signed back but wished she could speak. Her father, like many of the old ones, did not approve of the new way of communicating. The ways of the elders were the best ways. Gem and her friends disagreed but knew better than to argue.

"Good. I am hungry." He rubbed his rounded belly. His hunting vest gaped, showing his hair-covered upper body, and his hunting apron had slipped below his belly, barely covering his man parts. Her father ate well. He was not tall, but he was well rounded from her mother's and Gem's cooking.

Many of the cavemen were heavy bellied. They were allowed to eat first. They were the hunters. They were the ones who kept the clan alive. The women ate what was left, and if nothing was left when the men finished, the women would go to another fire and beg for food from the woman tending her fire.

No woman went hungry, and no child went hungry, but during the white months, it was very hard to keep everyone's bellies full.

Gem shuddered. Her father was not nice, nor was he pleasant to look upon. It was good she did not have to look at him very often. She thought about her mother, Ret. What did her mother find attractive about Tog? She would grant one thing—Tog was a good provider. Otherwise, he was a harsh, angry man.

"Sit, Father, and I will serve you," she signed, gesturing to his favorite pallet of furs. She knew he would flop down, spread his legs, and hold out his hands. She did not want to look at his shriveled man parts, but he never made an effort to cover them.

Men of the cave clan were not ashamed to show their men parts. Gem had seen the men sitting around one of the fires comparing their parts and lying about how well they satisfied their mates every night. Every man seemed to be so proud of his manhood.

Tog flopped down and did just as she had feared. *Ugh. Not nice.*

"It is cold tonight. I bring me another fur."

"Yes, Father, right away." She hurried to the rock shelf where her mother stored more fur rugs. Gem grabbed a long-furred ox rug and rushed to cover her father's legs and lap.

Now, his man parts were out of sight.

Tog nodded but didn't bother to sign his thanks. Since Gem was used to her father's manners, his attitude didn't bother her.

She shrugged and moved close to the fire.

Around her, throughout the cave, women prepared the evening meal at their own fires. Twelve families shared the winter quarters of her clan. Each family had its own niche carved into the sides of the massive main cave. The lucky ones resided in semi-privacy behind glistening shards hanging from the top of the cave.

She, her mother, and her father, one of the smaller families residing in the cave, were not so lucky. Their niche was near the open hole, which allowed the clan access to the world outside. It was a bad place in the white months. The cold wind blew through the opening, whipping around corners and moaning. Often, it was hard to keep the fire alive, especially when the wind was fierce.

Gem's father was a good hunter, and during the white time there were many furs to cover their bodies when they slept and many more furs to pile on the stone floor to keep their feet warm. Her mother had made all of them covering for their feet with the fur inside and the tanned skins outside to keep out the wet and cold when they went out into the weather.

Tec was sinking low in the sky and would soon disappear, leaving his sons to light the fires in the sky overhead.

The low hum of the many young voices begging for food from their harried mothers filled the air. Fires were being stoked. Men, who had been hunting all day, were returning to signed greetings and questions about their luck. With each returning man, the noise level rose. Babies, who had slept off and on all day, were awake and squalling for attention and food. The small children begged for attention from their fathers.

The cave echoed with the cacophony of sounds, some good, many annoying, and all of them a familiar part of Gem's life. Often, she wondered what it would be like to hear nothing but silence.

A cold breeze followed each man as he returned to the cave, making Gem wonder why one of the men didn't think to hang a heavy fur over the opening. Gem pondered how hard it would be to put one in place. It only made sense to her. The covering would keep so much of the cold air out, but she didn't dare suggest such an idea to the men.

If a man couldn't solve a problem, it was left unsolved.

Tog interrupted Gem's thoughts with a finger snap. "Where is your mother, girl?" he signed.

She cringed. If he didn't like her answer, he would think nothing of cuffing her. She handed him a large stone bowl filled to the brim with meat, gravy, and vegetables and crawled quickly out of arm's reach. She had learned early in life to stay out of harm's way. She found it easier to remain silent and submissive when her father was at the home-fire.

"Mother is in the bleeding room."

"Again?" Her father held out his bowl for more of the stew. His first bowlful had disappeared in a matter of moments.

Gem took the greasy bowl and nodded. It had been a full moon of days since her mother, Ret, had bled. A good husband would keep track of such things. Not Tog. He only thought about his own pleasure and pain.

It became clear the reason he'd asked for her mother was only about himself. Her father was a hunter. Today's hunt had gone well. He wanted to celebrate by dipping his man-shaft into her mother's woman's place.

Her father muttered a curse and threw his bowl aside. Gem wasn't surprised to see his hand go under the fur rug draped across his lap. She was sure he had his hand cupping his man-shaft. He would massage himself to ease the pain of want. Gem scooted further back into the shadows.

"She will be back in two passings of Tec across the sky," Gem assured him, trying not to show fear. If her father knew she feared him, it would only make him angrier. Anger was something the cave dwelling men expressed frequently, and when they did, it was an awesome sight.

The cave men were also not shy about exposing themselves to others. It was not unusual to see a man running through the cave with his man parts exposed searching for his mate to ease his shaft after a good day of hunting.

It was the way of life in the cave. Men became excited from the hunt, and their mates were there to ease the pain and hunger. If he could not find his mate, he might rub himself or ask another woman not mated to another to share her body.

If the woman was untried, he would have to pay her family to have use of her. It would be up to the woman to decide if she would play with him or not and one of the few decisions a woman was allowed to make for herself.

Though she had no mate yet, Gem understood men had needs and women had them, too. Her father's face reddened, and his hand moved faster. He was going to explode soon.

"Get your friend Cia," he growled at her. "She needs to fix this." He threw off the fur rug and pushed his hunting skirt out of the way, and his man-shaft stuck straight out, the swollen purple tip pointing at her. The sight of him made Gem's tummy hurt. At this moment, she hated him.

"No. I am busy." She shifted her feet and stared at the floor. Signing back to her father was not a good thing to do because she was inviting him to use his open hand on her face. She didn't care. Let him hit her. He was not going to use her sister-friend to service him. The thought gave her a queasy stomach, like bad meat. Why could he not take care of himself?

Her father grunted and searched the cave. Gem was not surprised when he settled upon Hoe, Cia's sister. She was sitting at the next fire over watching them. "Come here, girl, and help me," he demanded in a voice that echoed throughout the cave.

Hoe came running like a hungry pup. The young woman was fond of Tog and was always willing to relieve him of his baby-making juice when Gem's mother was bleeding.

Of course, it wasn't just Tog she serviced. Hoe liked to please many men. On a good hunting day, she was very busy.

Hoe squatted in front of the fully aroused man. Gem snuck a peek out of the corner of her eye. If his smile was any indication, Tog was glad to see Hoe. He leaned back, resting his elbows on the skins covering the floor. He gave Hoe a nod to indicate she should get on with her task.

Gem hated Hoe almost as much as she hated how her father acted when her mother was gone. Gem had made up her mind long ago that when she mated it would be for life, and she would not share her mate with anyone. He would be her man and no one else's. She would not share him with anyone. No other man or woman would be allowed to suck her mate. And, except for her mate, no other man would be allowed to taste or touch her. No other would share his baby-making juice. Every part of her mate would be hers and hers alone.

Gem had discussed her feelings with her mother and been told she was being selfish. Sharing was the only way to keep a mate happy. Men needed more than one woman to keep them content. Gem did not agree. She would keep her man so busy he would need no other besides her. She would see to it he was satisfied at all times.

Hoe was busy sucking Tog's shaft. Tog groaned and growled like a hungry bear as Hoe's head bobbed up and down, her lips tugging his knob. The whole business made Gem very angry.

She threw a large rug over them so she didn't have to watch them. It sickened her. Her father could at least have taken Hoe to another more private cave. There were several empty ones toward the back of the main cave.

Gem went on with her duties, ignoring the rising and falling of the fur rug in front of her. She wanted to laugh, but she also wanted to cry for her mother and the life most cave women led.

She turned her back to the rug and enjoyed her bowl of stew. The vegetables were just right. It had been worth the argument she'd had with the keeper of the vegetable cave. This day the keeper had been

Ke, the most obnoxious of all the cave-dwellers. Gem did not like dealing with Ke. She was old and thought she knew everything.

Today, Ke had wanted to discuss her beautiful son, Og. Gem did not want to talk about Og.

Her hunger for him was a secret she kept close to her heart. The last thing she wanted to do was talk about him with his mother.

Gem wanted to suckle Og's man-shaft until he exploded all over the cave, crowing and growling like an animal. He was the only man Gem would give her body to. Of all the men in this cave and the other caves in the hills around them, Og was the most talented hunter with the strongest body.

Not only did he have a wonderful body, Og was as beautiful as the sky above them when their god, Tec, made its way across to the darkside.

When no one was paying attention, Gem often wandered to Og's fire and tried to speak to him, but he always turned away.

She felt in her heart he was a good man because he helped his mother and seemed to like the small children who were always in the way. He never kicked the cave dogs, and she had seen him give his catch of the day to families in need. Yes, Og was a good man, always smiling and laughing. Except when she was near and then he, like her father, frowned and turned his back to her.

He was of age to choose a mate, yet he did not speak with any unmated women in the clan, not even Hoe or Gem's beautiful sister-friend, Cia.

He did not spend much time with the men of the cave, so he was not a man-lover. He was not a little boy at his mother's knee. In fact, he seldom spent time at his mother's fire. He'd moved to his own fire during the second white month the past winter because he had come of age.

Gem had seen Ke bragging to her friends Og would mate soon. He must have a girl in mind, because Ke said he was working on a dowry. Ke had admitted she didn't know who the woman was, but whomever he picked would be the best woman he could find.

Tog made a loud grunt. Gem made more noise cleaning up the cooking mess. She even managed to drop and shatter one of her mother's oldest cooking pots.

Gem would make her a new one. She felt bad, but anything was better than turning around and watching the bear rug move up and down.

Gem looked around the cave. Many dwellers were watching. Did her father have to be so disgusting? If only he would go somewhere else. The whole thing made her sick to her stomach. The couple continued to play. Gem wanted to laugh. The long-haired fur blanket looked silly as it wiggled up and down. She didn't want to know what was going on under it and hoped Hoe would go home soon. Gem finished sand scrubbing the stone bowls. If only she didn't have to live with her parents. She couldn't wait until she could choose a mate and get away from her father's fire. When she was done cleaning the bowls, she neatened their niche.

Yes, Gem tried to ignore their grunts and cries, but her mind wouldn't let her. She wanted Og with all her body, and the noises her father and Hoe were making only served to remind Gem how much she wanted to be Og's mate. How much she cared for him. How much she wanted Og.

Gem took a small stick and drew on the ground. She wanted to design a new pot to replace the one she had broken. It was hard to find stone soft enough to carve out the insides yet remain strong enough to cook in. She would go looking for the right stone tomorrow.

Gem sighed. Hoe was making a lot of noise.

Hoe didn't talk much, but she was very vocal when mating. She left little to the imagination.

Hoe was always bragging about how the men admired her baby-feeders. Yes, they were large, but one day they would droop to the ground like all the old women. Then Hoe would be nothing special and it would serve her right for being a showoff.

Cia called baby-feeders titties or teats. She said it was easier to say, and Gem agreed. Besides, they were used for much more than feeding babies. The men seemed to like them and were often pinching or licking their mate's teats.

Gem lay awake many nights wondering what it would be like to have Og suck and nip her titties.

Gem wanted to leave the fire, but go where? She searched the cave for a sign of Og. She was tired of waiting for him to take her to mate. Her body and tits ached to be nipped and suckled.

She was so hungry for Og's mouth on her body, his man-shaft in her woman's place. Why was he always avoiding her? Every time Gem tried to catch Og's attention, he pretended not to see her, or he turned his back. Worst of all were the times when Og told her to leave him because he was busy.

This very rising of Tec, Og's mother, Ke, had boldly reminded her that her son was the most beautiful man in the cave, and he was too good for the likes of Gem. He had every unattached girl in their clan and other nearby clans to choose from. He did not need Gem. Why should he choose her?

Seated, she didn't see his glorious golden hair reflecting anywhere in the main cave, so she stood and scanned all the fire-pits. At last she spied him hunched over his own fire-pit.

From what Ke had signed earlier in the day, Gem thought Og would be eating his evening meal at his mother's fire.

She stood silently rocking back and forth on her soft, fur-lined boots. She had waited long enough. She wanted Og, and she was going to have him. As for her father, he could take a flying leap off the ledge at the opening of the main cave.

* * * *

Og didn't bother to look up. He had smelled her long before she squatted on the other side of his fire. Her scent was a combination of the large flowers floating in the cool pond and the sweet fruit that covered the trees in hot days.

Gem. Beautiful Gem. His man-shaft strengthened, filling with life-giving juices. His balls tightened against his body. He wanted her so much. But first he had to ask her father for her, and Tog was not an easy man to hunt with or spend any passing of Tec. Tog was a brutal hunter and often destroyed the hides of his catch.

Og did not look forward to signing with Tog and avoided him whenever possible. Tog was as hardheaded as a wild boar and twice as ugly. Once his mind was made up, the negotiations were over.

Tog had placed a high price on his daughter's body. Then he issued a dare and a warning to every unmated man in their cave and the caves surrounding the valley to pay the price or forget about taking Gem for a mate. He wanted many antelope hides for his beautiful only child.

Og had been hunting for many passings of Tec, and he had killed everything from antelope to tiger, knowing antelope hides would not be enough to satisfy Tog. Og usually let his mother do most of the work on his hides, but this time he did not trust her. He had tanned each hide carefully, folded it gently, and stacked it, along with the others he'd cured in the corner of the carved niche where he slept. The pile was growing each day. In fact, it was now so large, he'd been sleeping wrapped in a bear skin near his fire-pit. Soon, he would have enough wealth to approach Tog.

He took a deep breath and savored the scent of Gem. The sweetness of flowers and honey filled his nostrils, and his man-shaft trembled. Her scent drove him crazy. No other woman in this cave or any other cave smelled as good as Gem. He knew this because he had spent many days sniffing other women, nuzzling their necks and licking noses only to be disappointed. They smelled like dirt or the hides they wore. Whatever their scent, Og was always disappointed.

The women were all unpleasant. Gem's scent was enough to make the juices in his mouth and shaft start flowing.

Sweet Gem.

"Og?" Her soft voice tickled his ears. He liked when she spoke to him and didn't sign.

"Mmm?"

"Can we speak?"

He looked up and willed his man-shaft to stay hidden. "Why?"

Her hair, the color of clouds on a hot day, fell over her face in long waves. She brushed it back and he could see her sky-blue eyes. They were softer than a doe's, and often they said far more than her lips.

If anyone saw them talking, it could cause trouble. The old ones didn't approve of speaking in words. Even worse, Og was staring into Gem's eyes. It was not proper, but he couldn't stop himself. Her eyes were so pretty and expressive. The things her eyes whispered made his shaft tingle.

"Because…" Gem said.

He turned his eyes from hers and tried not to smile. He picked up a handful of sand and went back to working on the saber-toothed tiger skin he'd been tanning for many nights. "Can't you see I am busy, girl?"

Her pale skin turned pink. "Yes, I see you are busy. You can talk and work, can you not?"

"Hmm." He growled and brushed the sand off the hide, shook it, and Gem jumped back. Sand flew in many directions and settled on Gem's head. She'd covered her eyes with a hand, for which Og was relieved. He did not want to hurt her. He only wanted t her to leave before he exploded baby-making juice all over.

Maybe she would leave if he continued working and ignored her.

He stood, grabbed the huge skin, and walked to the cave opening. He could feel her eyes watching his every move. He unrolled the skin and shook the sand off. Some of it blew back and stuck to his sweat-dampened chest and in his eyes.

Tec!

He was a mess. Would it matter to her? Would she finally leave him to his work?

Back at his fire-pit she was kneeling, waiting.

Og flipped the tiger skin fur side down on the ground. He squatted and reached into a deep stone bowl next to him, pulling out a mixture of entrails and ash his mother had made for him.

Gem shifted slightly but didn't move.

The disgusting stench of the mixture did nothing to cover the womanly scent of her. Og sighed. It was good to know the woman he wanted as a mate was not going to let a handful of rotting entrails chase her away.

Still, it would ease his aching shaft if she would leave him alone. He stared at her, and she met his eyes. Her eyes sparkled, and she smiled. Her teeth were as shining as Tec and as bright as her cloud-colored hair. Most of the clan women used their teeth to chew skins thin enough to use as a travois. They chewed, bones, wood, whatever they needed to make something. . The bones were chewed and carved with obsidian to make sturdy, small tools to sew skins together for clothing. The wood was used to draw on after it had been chewed many passings of Tec to break down the fiber. Then the women spread out the mass in the shining of Tec and left it to dry. Small branches made fine writing tools. The children used small pieces of burned wood to draw on the dried wood mash. The clan artists drew animals and people on the cave walls using a concoction of herbs, oils, and ground charcoal.

All the chewing usually wore the woman teeth down to brown nubs in their mouths. It was not nice to look at. But Og couldn't fault the women for they worked hard every day.

The women of the clan were very smart and hard working.

It was not something the men liked to talk about, but it was true. The men were great hunters, but the cave women were the keepers of history with drawings. The women made sure the men and children were fed. A cave could not function without its women.

Og admired Gem. She was beautiful, smart, and talented. She had been taught well by her mother and the other women of the clan in the ways of the ancients and their healing skills. She would make a good mate. Not to mention she had all her teeth. Her slender, sturdy body and her bright teeth made her a prize well worth every skin Og could find to appease her father.

Oh, help me, Tec, Og pleaded silently. I'm going to take her now.

"Go away, girl. I am busy." He threw the handful of rotting entrails on the skin, picked up a sharp stone, and began scrapping on the tiger skin, taking care not to push or pull too hard and make a hole in the fine skin.

Gem squatted at the head of the tiger and watched him intently. In order to see better, she leaned close, and Og began to tremble. She had pulled up the long winter garment that flowed around her lower half, giving him a clear view of her long, slender legs. She did not use the thick, fur leggings and short skirt covers like other men and women but wore a wrap of fine, woven fibers.

She was the only woman in the cave who dressed in the soft garment. Her mother, Ret, had hunkered down next to her fire for many passings of Tec and worked with the soft fur of the cave dogs to make the coverings worn by her beautiful daughter.

His mother, Ke, felt Gem and some of the other girls showed too much of their bodies before they were mated, but Og did not agree. He liked watching the young women working in the cave wearing very little.

He and the other young men cheered when the young women walked past taking steps hard enough to make their baby-feeders jiggle. He sat with the other men only in hopes of seeing Gem walk past. But she was very careful to keep her body covered and walk lightly.

Og had a secret. He spied on Gem and her sister-friend, Cia, when they bathed in the warm pool.

Tonight, Gem was showing more of her body than normal. She didn't know he was watching her.

Og was scrapping the skin so hard, she had to be thinking he was simply working on a skin for a new cover for his mother.

She'd shown Og her legs. Would she show him her baby-feeders? If he hadn't been watching, he would have missed the flash of her flushed skin. She leaned even closer, and her covering dipped, giving him a clear view of her creamy skin. Her baby-feeders were large and rosy-tipped.

Shame made him forget for a moment what he was supposed to be doing. Gem gave him a strange look.

"Are you ill, Og?"

"No."

She had no idea how often he had followed her and her sister-friend, Cia, to the bathing pool. Gem was so beautiful, he couldn't stop spying on the girls. He would watch impatiently for Gem to bare her slim body, long, strong legs, and large baby-feeders.

Cia was also unusually beautiful and smart. Og didn't understand why he wasn't interested in her. He only had eyes for Gem.

Not only had he watched her in the heated pool, he'd watched her running like a gazelle across the valley. It was a wonderful sight to see. She ran naked with her hair streaming behind her. Watching her made his shaft rise every time. It was agony to watch and not join her.

Every step long and perfect. Her arms moving in harmony with her feet and legs. Her baby-feeders taut against her body. She was more beautiful than the sky when Tec settled behind the cliffs.

She was going to make him a wonderful mate. They would hunt together. They would lay under a large tree, open the sack she had made, and they would eat a mid-day meal. They would mate many times, and then they would continue their hunt.

It was difficult to keep control of his body when he watched her bathe, wash her silky hair in the pool, or run with the wind. He wasted a lot of his juices on the ground.

One day soon, he would no longer waste his juices. He would be filling his mate, Gem.

"Og," Gem whispered.

She was leaning too close. Og inhaled, and his shaft grew.

"What?" He tried to not sound angry. He wasn't. He was hungry for her. Hungry to taste her and lick her all over.

"Will you tell me about hunting this tiger?" She smiled.

"No. I do not have time. Why do you not listen to me? I am busy, girl. Go away." He did not like treating her harshly, but until he had enough hides to please her father, he would have to. All he could do was hope she would not become angry enough to stop bothering him and go to another man's cave.

Og shuffled around until his back was to her. She did not go away. Her scent was still in the air around him.

"Please, Og," she begged. "Talk to me. I will only listen. I will not speak."

He looked up to see her standing in front of him. Og shrugged a shoulder. "No time."

She spread her long legs open, and he could see the soft hair guarding her woman parts. Her scent surrounded him. He could barely stop himself from leaping on her and jamming his man-shaft into her untried body. No, the first time would have to be gentle. He did not want to hurt her or injure her. Mating with her would be like flying through the air with the tiny winged animals that made music.

Everyone in the cave knew she was ripe for the taking because her father, Tog, bragged about it all the time to any man who would listen. Tog wanted to sell her soon. She was now eighteen summers, and Tog did not want to wait much longer. It was time she left her father's fireside and started her own family.

Tog had been threatening to take Gem to other caves. Her mother cried whenever the subject came up. The other caves were too far away. She might not see Gem very often. Tog had growled and signed it was time to find out if any man was interested in her. Every time Og had noticed Tog signing to his friends about taking Gem to other caves, he became sick with worry. Why couldn't her father wait a few more weeks?

Og worried. If he didn't have enough skins to impress a man of such importance in the cave hierarchy as Tog, he would lose Gem to some fool from another cave.

Please, Tec, don't let Tog give her away!

Og wanted Gem for his own.

"I talked to your mother today," Gem tried again. "She spoke of you."

Og waved her off. "She speaks of me to everyone." She also lectured Og on a daily basis, telling him it was time for him to take a mate. He had not told her of his plans to offer for Gem because his mother did not approve of Gem. Og had a feeling his mother would never agree to accept any woman as his mate. She might tell him it was time to mate, but she always shook her head when Og mentioned a woman's name.

One was too fat, one too stupid, one too lazy, one ugly, another had bad teeth, one had been mated three times and every one of her mates had died. His mother was adamant that woman was not coming near her beautiful son.

Once he casually brought up Gem's name, and his mother had ignored him for seven passings of Tec.

Gem inched toward him, and Og backed up so fast he nearly lost his balance. If her father saw them too close together, he would blow up. Her father had been known to flatten a man with one blow.

"I prepared a large meal tonight." Gem's gentle voice interrupted his thoughts. "Are you hungry?"

He was starving. Not for food but for her. "My mother has fed me."

Gem laughed softly. "You lie. I know she no longer makes your meals. Come sit at our fire and eat. You are working too hard."

"I said I am busy, girl. Go back to your fire-pit."

Her shoulders drooped, and her smile disappeared.

He felt lower than the lowest cave dog snuffling the ground for bones. He had hurt her, which was the last thing he wanted, but it couldn't be helped. She had to leave. Now.

She turned, but not before he saw tears gather in the corners of her eyes. He watched her walk away and ached to call her back.

If he called her back and laid her on his bear skin, her father would demand double payment for her. If Og took her maidenhead, Tog would demand Og be turned out of the caves without a spear or club. Without the protection of cave and clan, Og might be killed by the beasts roaming the valley. If he was very lucky, he might be taken in by another clan, but if they knew why he'd been turned out of his own cave, they could refuse him the safety of their cave.

He was used to his comforts—a warm fire and plenty of pelts to cover him when he slept.

None of the alternatives were appealing.

Despite the fact he had Tog's anger on his mind, Og couldn't stop thinking about Gem's body, and his man-shaft would not go back to hiding between his legs. His shaft pulsed and throbbed, begging for release. He slipped his hand inside his deer-skin wrap to stroke his shaft. He imagined it was Gem's small hand wrapped around him, caressing him, and minutes later, his juice sprayed onto the cave floor. Much relieved, he returned to scrapping the tiger skin.

* * * *

Rejected again.

Gem walked across the cave and squatted next to Cia and Hoe's mother, Fa. Fa and her husband, Dec, had seen at least forty summers come and go. Their great age made them revered among the cave people. The fact Fa was with child made her even more revered by the people.

Gem used a finger to designate each child Fa had given birth to and realized there were more than the fingers on her one hand. No wonder she was held in high esteem. Especially since all of them had survived. Many children seldom lived past the time they toddled around the cave. There were many accidents with the fire-pits, a few minutes' lack of attention and a baby would wander out of the cave and tumble down the rock walls. Sickness and hunger during the white time were also the enemy of babies.

Fa, like some of the old dwellers, refused to speak with her mouth and would only use hand signs. Gem's grandmother, Pet, had taught Gem the signals when she was a child, but she did not like to sign. It was easier to use words. The gestures were slow and annoying, but if it made the elders happy, so be it. Gem and Cia spent a lot of time with other young cave dwellers making up new words for things. Because Cia was one of the smartest young women in the clan, Gem often asked for her help deciding if a word would be useful.

Gem approached Fa's fire without looking anyone in the eye. She squatted in front of her friend's mother and signed, "Where is Cia?"

Fa's fingers flew, and Gem had a hard time keeping up with the older woman. Fa didn't answer her question about Cia. Instead, she had many questions regarding the health of Gem's mother. When Fa found out Ret was bleeding again, she frowned and shook her head.

Gem was fast losing patience. She was anxious to talk to Cia. She'd thought of a word for accepting a man's shaft and wanted to see if Cia would like the word. It was important to get her approval. The old ones said one day, depending on who she chose to mate with, Cia would be head of her own clan.

Fa ignored Gem's desire to find Cia and signed for Gem to join her in a cup of herbal tea.

Gem made herself comfortable by spreading two folded animal pelts over a large rock. She left part of the pelt on the cave floor so her bottom would not get cold. She snuggled down into the furs and accepted the bowl of steaming liquid. She tried not to wrinkle her nose. The brew smelled horrible.

Fa signed for her to drink. It would keep her health and help her sleep.

Ah. Sleep. Something Gem had not been able to do of late. Maybe it would give her a night without thoughts of Og or it might keep the dream-weaver away. Gem dreamed about Og every night. In every dream, he was her mate. In every dream, he was about to put his man-shaft into her body, and she would jerk awake with tears on her face.

Beautiful Og.

Some days, all Gem could think about was Og's man-shaft stirring under his deer-skin wrap. Too many nights, her thoughts were of Og and how large and handsome his shaft was. He wasn't like other men in the cave who walked about without covering, searching for a woman. She'd only seen glimpses of his shaft when he headed to the scat room every morning. She often thought about how he would feel filling her woman place.

She wondered what his shaft and creamy juices would taste like. Cia said a man's juices tasted of the salts around the pool to the west of the cave, and it was as rich and white as Gem's hair.

Fa tapped Gem on the knee, and she jumped. She hadn't realized she'd drifted off in thought.

Fa pressed her to drink while the brew was hot, and Gem nodded.

She blew on the liquid and took a careful sip. It was disgusting. She tried not to make a face and offend Fa. She signed her thanks and told Fa it was fragrant but strong.

Fa's fingers flew. Gem sat the bowl of drink on the cave floor and tried to stand up. Fa stopped her and gestured to finish the drink. Fa asked again about Gem's mother, Ret. Gem tried to keep up with Fa, but it was very confusing.

Eventually, Gem figured out Fa wanted to know if Tog was doing his duty to his mate. Gem told her about Hoe, but Fa waved her hand as if chasing a small biting bug away. It wasn't important. Fa also asked if Ret had been taking the herbs she'd been given. Gem nodded.

Fa was not happy to hear Ret was crying all the time. Crying wasted energy and did not make a woman's body receptive to baby-making seeds. It made Fa very sad to know her friend was bleeding again. She told Gem there was nothing more she could do for Ret. She'd used all her potions and herbs. Maybe it was Tog, and if so, there would be no baby.

Fa knew much about making babies. It was also whispered she knew how to keep from having a baby. Gem hoped the whispers were true because when she mated with Og, she didn't want to share him with anyone for a very long time.

Fa was the one the cave dwellers called upon when it was time for a new baby to join the clan. No birth was too hard or complicated for Fa. She knew all the secrets of a woman's insides and had often told the women of the clan no birth was too dangerous for her to handle, and so far she'd been right.

Fa was teaching several of the young clan women her secrets, so they could take over when she was too old to continue to help the women.

Gem thought her mother was too old for another child. Besides, Gem liked being her mother's only child, and Gem wasn't too sure her father wanted another child, either. Not when he went around spilling his seed playing with Hoe all the time.

Hoe had mated with many of the cavemen and had not rounded with a baby. It could be Fa was helping her daughter with one of her secrets. Gem was going to have to talk with Cia about Fa's secrets.

Cia suddenly appeared from nowhere. "Gem! I'm glad you are here, because I wanted to talk."

Gem smiled. "I, too, my sister." She gestured toward Fa. "I have a hard time talking with your mother."

Cia laughed, and the soft trill echoed through the cave. Several men looked up from their fires. Cia was unmated but not untried. Many men vied for her hand, and all had been turned away by Cia and her father.

Fa handed Cia a bowl of herbal tea. Her hands told the younger women she was tired, and with a short, sharp wave she disappeared into her sleeping cave.

"So?" Cia asked, taking a sip of the hot tea. "Ugh! Nasty!"

The two friends had made up the word "nasty" when Fa had served them a strange vegetable they had never had before. The vegetable became squishy in their mouths and left a bad taste. The word "nasty" was perfect.

Gem took a sip from her bowl. The herbal drink was now cool and tasted even worse. "Yuck!"

They giggled softly so as not to anger Fa. The baby in her belly made her tired and irritable. Sleep would do her good. With another giggle, Cia took the bowl from Gem's hand and emptied it into a corner. She sanded the bowls and stacked them next to the fire-pit.

Gem stood, spreading the pelts she'd been leaning against onto the cave floor. She held out her arms, and Cia came into them readily. They lay down and twined themselves around each other like mating snakes. For a few moments, they watched the fire shimmer and dim before Cia whispered, "Do you want me to do your hair?" She ran her slender fingers through Gem's hair

Gem shook her head. "Not tonight. Tomorrow, we will go to the hot pool and you can wash and comb it for me."

Cia left her fingers in Gem's hair and tugged her head close. She rubbed her nose on Gem's and blew a gentle breath into her friend's mouth. When Gem opened her lips, Cia touched her lips to Gem's. Pulling away, Cia asked, "Why are you here?"

Gem smiled. "I wanted to play."

"So do I." Cia's hand slipped into the top of Gem's covering and cupped her teat. "Nice."

"Um-hum." Gem wiggled to get closer to her friend. Cia began playing with the tip, and Gem whimpered. "Wait, I thought of a new word, and I wanted to ask if you liked it or not."

"Really?" Cia snuggled back down next to Gem.

"Yes. I thought of a word for a man-shaft."

"A better one?"

Gem nodded. "Yes, and another word for putting a man-shaft into a woman's secret place."

"Ooh. Good. I have a word for woman's secret place."

Her friend was almost as beautiful as Og. She ran a finger over Cia's teat. "I like your titties. They are so big."

"Your titties are bigger and prettier than mine," Cia said, covering Gem's full teat with her hand.

Sighs filled the quiet as they continued to caress each other. Cia flicked a finger over Gem's teat, and Gem moaned at the good feelings.

"Tell me your words," Cia said. d.

"I think we should call a man-shaft a cock," Gem managed to say between moans.

Cia mulled the word over several times, rolling the sound over her tongue until Gem began to giggle. "Cock. C–c–c–cock. C–o–o–o–o–ck. I like it," Cia finally decided.

Gem grinned. "I think putting a cock in a woman should be 'fuck.' What do you think?"

"Fuck. Fucking. F–f–f–f–f–fucked." Cia laughed. "What about 'cunt' for a woman's special place? Do you like cunt?"

"I like cunt very much. It is nice." While they spoke of cocks and cunts, Cia and Gem touched one another, laughing and playing. It was the way of many unmated women in the clan. Some of the men mated each other. It was an acceptable practice. The play trained both young men and women how to please a mate, and it eased the call to mate before they were old enough.

Cia cupped Gem's heavy teats in her hands. "I will lick now, yes?"

Gem nodded. Cia's mouth was hot and wet on her titties and made her cunt ache, but as much as she cared for Cia, Gem wished it was Og sucking on her.

How much longer was Og going to be too busy? She had thrown herself at him tonight, and he had been so rude. Was he blind? He must have seen her cunt. She had been open and wet for him, and yet he sent her away, pretending he had not looked between her legs. He had even stared into her eyes for a moment when she had first joined him at his fire.

Only mates and warriors were supposed to look into one another's eyes. Did he want to fight her or fuck her?

Cia slipped a finger into Gem's wet cunt, and Gem gasped against Cia's smooth neck. She licked her friend's brown skin and whimpered.

"Good," she said. Yes. it was good, but it would be even better if it was Og's cock there and not Cia's fingers.

Cia continued to touch her cunt and the sensitive spot growing and swelling under her friend's fingers. Gem's insides quaked, and her cunt sucked against Cia's fingers.

She lifted her hips and rocked against her friend's fingers, cooing, "Yes. Yes. Yes."

Cia moved her fingers faster and faster until Gem was shaking, her body moving like the earth when the volcano erupted. Flowers of pleasure opened inside her, and she closed her eyes and imagined Og.

When she caught her breath, Gem helped Cia achieve the same release. Then the two friends pulled a heavy skin over themselves, the fire to their backs, and fell asleep.

* * * *

Morning brought with it the usual noise associated with cave dwelling.

Several sleeping caves away, little Loc started to cry. His mother stuffed his mouth with her teat, but she wasn't fast enough. Before long, other babies began to sob, reminding mothers they needed to be fed before anything else could be done.

The massive cave brightened as more fires were stoked, and the women, babies slung inside carrying sacks at the waist, began cooking for their men. Soon the men would leave to hunt, and their bodies needed fuel to fight through the cold and track the animals. It would be at least one more moon before the weather would warm enough to make hunting easier.

Gem rolled over, using Cia as a pillow, and watched the cave become a beehive of activity. Soon, Fa would kick them and order them to get up. Fa was always crabby in the mornings. Gem suspected it was because she was not resting with the baby so large and heavy in her belly. Not to mention the fact her mate used her nightly to relieve his cock.

For the moment, Gem enjoyed the scene, and she was even happier when Og trotted past on his way to the scat cave.

As he ran past each fire, the golden fur on his chest and legs picked up the light and made him look exactly like the god Tec crossing the sky. She sighed. If only he would come closer so she could push back his clothing and fondle his cock. Would he like the new words, cock and fuck? Would he let her touch him? Would he ever want to touch her?

Hoe was not by the fire. She must have slept the night with Tog. If the greedy girl had been in the main cave, Gem had no doubt she would have chased after Og. Hoe made no secret of her desire for Ke's golden son to be her mate. She told everyone any time the beautiful man's name was mentioned.

Gem told no one but Cia how she felt about Og. Gem decided to be brave. She sat up and pushed aside the cloth covering her teats.

"Og," she called out to him softly. She leaned back, resting her hands flat on the bear rug, arching her back so her titties stuck out, large and firm. She looked down at herself and was pleased to see the pink tips were hard. Og had to be blind to not notice how pretty her teats were today.

"What?" Og stopped, his expression somewhere between curious and wary.

Look at me, she begged silently. See how pretty my teats are this day.

Og ignored her silent urging and stared past her, focusing on the stone wall behind her.

Anger made her voice sharp. "Stop for a time and talk to me."

Og scratched his bare toe in the dirt covering the stone floor. He fidgeted, and his hand dropped to hover over his crotch, as if hiding something there.

Gem felt a giggle building up in her chest. He was nervous! His face was red. Was it from running, or was he afraid to look at her?

"I cannot stop today. I am busy." He lowered his eyes to hers.

Finally. Excitement shot through her like the pleasure of Cia's touch.

"Please?" It didn't seem right a mere man could be as beautiful as Og yet deny himself to all women and all men as well. Her fingers twitched, aching to cover his shaft. If only she could tangle her fingers in the fur guarding his cock and stroke his length. She would take him in her mouth and suck him dry. If only...

"Later, girl. I am busy." He took off at a slow lope, and Gem's heart flipped at the sight of his hard, muscular behind shifting as he jogged.

Next to Gem, Cia jolted, cried out, and scrambled from the fur rug.

Gem jerked around to see Fa's foot raised to kick Cia again. Gem stifled a bubble of laughter. This morning had started like nearly every other, but then Og had looked into her eyes. Perhaps something else new would happen today.

When Fa turned her angry gaze on Gem, Gem jumped up and twitched her woven covering back in place. She did not feel like facing Fa's ire so early in the day. Fa might not use words, but she could certainly make herself clear. Laziness was not something Fa tolerated, nor did she like the young women teasing the men on their way to the scat cave.

Gem wished Fa and Cia a good day and ran back to her home-fire before her father woke. She built the fire back up, adding several pieces of wood, and when the flame was hot, she carefully laid in a piece of black rock. The cave dwellers called the black rock coal. Long ago, someone had found the rock by accident, and now it was revered by all for the heat it gave for hours.

Gem sat a hand-carved stone pot on the edge of the fire and began warming the previous night's stew. She also put a pot of water on the cooking stone, and when bubbles formed in the water, she threw in the dark brown nuts she had gathered a season ago and dried. The brew simmered at the very edge of the fire.

Tog crawled out from under the bear rug and squatted beside her. His cock and balls dangled between his legs, and he scratched the curly, dark hair surrounding his shaft. For a moment, Gem was reminded of the small furry animals living in the forest trees.

She knew better than to laugh. Her father would box her ears.

"I am going to the scat cave, and when I return, my food will be ready and Hoe will be gone." Tog never asked Gem to have his meal ready. He ordered it. When Og was her mate, he would ask her to prepare the meal, and if he boxed her ears for anything, she would not suck his cock until he was sorry.

Gem kept one eye on her father's meal and one eye out for Og. A short time later, she caught sight of his golden body rushing past. As often happened when he was anywhere near her, Gem's cunt became moist and hot for his cock. Would he ever notice her with the same kind of longing she felt for him?

Hoe must have heard her moving around and clambered from under the bear rug. She was naked and rosy from sleep. Just as Og raced past, Hoe made a show of stretching and caressing her baby-feeders.

Gem was surprised Og continued on as if he didn't see Hoe's beautiful body. Hoe didn't seem too happy. She yanked her hunting skirt out from under the rug and strapped it on with a grunt. Gem was sure Hoe had said a bad word but hadn't quite heard it.

Relief flooded Gem's tense body when Hoe stomped back to her own family fire-pit.

For a moment, Gem thought Hoe would follow him, but she had gone home instead.

Gem was pouring a small bowlful of nut brew when Tog returned to the fireside. "Good day to you, Father," Gem said with proper subservience, handing him the bowl. She knew her place at this fireside, and she couldn't wait to have her own fire because it would mean she was no longer a slave to her father's bad moods.

"Ungh," he grunted in response. Tog took the scalding brew, sipped, smiled, and signed, "Good."

Eyes turned toward the cave floor, Gem nodded. She handed him a large bowl of stew and watched in amazement as he stuffed his mouth, chewed, swallowed, and smacked his lips.

"More," Tog's fingers demanded, holding out his empty bowl.

Gem filled his bowl once again and hoped there would be enough for her own morning meal. Her belly growled at each bite Tog took.

Tog finished his meal, tossed the empty bowl aside, and scratched his belly, setting his cock and balls into motion. Gem would be glad when he put his hunting cover on and left the cave. She hated it when he scratched his balls and played with his cock. To use one of her new words, it was nasty.

Tog stood and went into the sleeping cave, returning in moments, his leggings on and his hunting cover in hand. He wrapped his hunting cover and fastened it with a sinew string. He shoved his arms through the armholes of the hardened leather chest cover her mother had made for him and picked up his spear and club.

"I will return," Tog said.

Gem nodded and smiled at the earthen floor. Tog's farewell always sounded like a threat.

Familiar footsteps had her sneaking a peek out the corner of her eye. It was Og, carrying his own spear and club. He, too, wore his hunting cover, leggings, and a cloak of sturdy furs made by Ke.

Gem sighed. As always, Og was larger than life. His muscular arms bulged, and the chest cover barely contained his upper body. His golden hair flowed down his back in waves like a waterfall flowing over the cliffs.

Gem lifted a hand and hoped he would stop. Her belly dipped and her insides quivered when he did. Gem thanked Tec Hoe had gotten angry and gone home.

Gem, feeling braver than she had earlier, smiled when she realized Og was staring directly at her for what seemed like one full moon but was only a flick of time. Would he speak?

"Gem," he said, smiling at her for the first time in days, "I will be back."

Thank you, Tec. Gem sighed and smiled at the floor. "Good. Then we will talk, yes?"

Og laughed. As always, the husky sound made her cunt weep. "If I am not too busy," he said with a broad grin.

"Oooh." This time it was true. After the hunt, he would have to clean and dress out the animal or animals he killed. He was one of the greatest, most fearless hunters in the whole valley and well known for his skills.

"Good day." He lifted his spear, shouting as he did, "Eouwww!" And, in a flash of bright light, he was gone.

* * * *

White clouds of peaceful steam rose into the air and surrounded the young women in a cloak of secrecy.

"Get in," Cia said, giving Gem a friendly push on the back.

Gem pulled off her cloth covering and, taking care to plant her feet firmly on the rocks, stepped into the pool, carrying her covering in one hand. Her mother had woven her several of the soft coverings, so she had a fresh one to slip on after her bath. Later, she would set the wet one to dry at the fireside.

Cia pulled off her tanned deer-skin covering, stepped into the heated pool, and sat next to Gem. "This is nice. Yes?"

Gem laughed, splashing her friend with warm water. "Yes."

"Let's play." Cia tugged at Gem's hand.

"In a moment. I need to scrub my covering."

Cia lifted the soft woven fabric in her fingers. "I thought of a word for it this morning."

"Oh?"

"Yes. It is a dress."

"Dress? Good, but it sounds like a snake."

"It is a dress." Cia pushed Gem, and she slipped under the water.

Gem came up laughing and spluttering. "Dress. You are right. It is a dress."

This was their pool. Gem had found it a short run from the cave and had not told the elders. Let them find their own pools. There were many in the valley, several of them full of hot, clear water, others with cool, clean water. Others were full of hot, bubbling dark, smelly stuff.

They enjoyed the freedom of the early morning. The air was cold, but the pool was warm. The steam gave them the privacy they craved after living in the confines of the cave with its noise and confusion.

Eventually, Gem finished washing her dress, and they scrubbed each other's bodies and hair with herbs smelling of the fruits of summer. They foamed like the bubbles where the waterfall hit the river. Gem had a growing knowledge of various herbs and other gifts of the earth. Ret and Fa had trained her in the ways of herbs and medicine so she could one day become the medicine woman for the cave-dwellers. Ret said she would not live forever, and the cave-dwellers would need a medicine woman to heal the hurts of the men.

Gem slicked her hair off her face. Laughing, she turned her face to the god, Tec, who warmed her and dried her face with loving fingers. Just as Og warmed her heart.

Beautiful, golden-furred Og. Would he be busy after the hunt? Would he have time for her?

"Cia?"

Cia's face was also turned up to Tec. "Yes, my sister?"

"Why is Og always busy?"

Cia laughed. "I do not know. When I ask him, he never says he is busy, but he doesn't stop to talk to me, either. He smiles and hurries away. I don't think he is interested in me, and that is good since you want him for yourself."

Gem sighed. "When I try to talk to him, the only thing he ever says is he is busy."

Cia twisted her long, dark hair, wringing out the water. "He is a busy man. Soon, he might be chief of his own cave, just as I will be chief of my own cave."

Gem's stomach churned, and she stared at her true friend. "Sister? Do you want him for your mate?" What would she do if Cia wanted Og? She had always considered him her mate. If Cia took him for mate, Gem would have to throw herself off the cliff. She shivered and wrapped her arms around her body, squeezing herself tightly.

"No." Cia placed a finger on the tip of Gem's teat. "You know well I want Let. He is as beautiful as the night. He is strong with mighty thighs, a tight bottom, and a large cock with heavy balls. He will make many strong babies."

Both young women giggled. It was true. Let's backside was as tight and firm as Og's and just as handsome.

Cia stopped giggling and covered her mouth for a moment. "His cock is thick and dark. His balls are heavy with treasure."

Gem nodded. She had seen Let running for the scat cave many mornings, and he was large. Very large. Maybe not quite as large as Og, but close. "Yes, he is big. Will it matter to anyone that his skin is not like ours?"

Cia frowned. "No one has ever cared about his skin color, so I think it will not matter. It is one thing making him special among us and one of the reasons I want him for a mate. No one will have as beautiful a mate as I have. Except perhaps you, Gem."

Gem nodded. "He is as brown as the nuts I use to brew my father's morning drink. His face is without hair as is his body, except for the guardians of his cock."

Cia smiled. "His shaft is mighty and very dark. His balls are full and hang heavy. His seed will be as sweet as the flowers of the field and will be filled with many babies." Gem smiled. "But, my sister, he does not smile very often."

Cia agreed. "True, but when he does, his teeth gleam like Tec on a bright, white day. Have you noticed when he stands sometimes, from the side, he seems to be carved from stone?"

"The hair on his head is different also, my sister. I've never seen hair on other men like his. It is so dark and curled tight against his head..."

"The few times I have touched his hair, the curls were soft as the hair on a baby."

"I have seen him with the cave children, and he is gentle and kind. Not like some of the men who shove the little ones out of the way or walk right over them if they get away from their mother's side. He is like Og. A good man."

"Yes. He will be a good leader because he is a gentle man."

"Then why do you wait so long, my sister?"

"You know I had to wait until he was eighteen summers. So I have waited. And finally he is of age."

"You have waited a long time." "Yes, since we were children."

Gem studied her friend. "Sister?"

"Yes?"

"You have pleasured other men of the cave. You cannot claim to be untried when you mate."

"I haven't done it often…"

"No, but does Let feel anger when you join with other men?" Gem asked.

Cia laughed, and the rich sound filled the air. "No. He knows I only want him, but he also knew he was too young. I am only pleasuring others to learn more so I can please Let."

"I see." Gem nodded in agreement. Perhaps she should be giving herself to other men to gain more knowledge so she could please Og when he was finally not "busy."

"Cia?"

"Yes, what is it?"

"Does it hurt?"

"You mean the first time you fuck Og?"

Gem could tell her cheeks were red. She put her hands on them to cool the burning. "Yes."

"It only hurts a little."

"How little?"

Cia pinched Gem's arm, and Gem squeaked. "Ow."

Cia laughed. "It will hurt only a moment, and then it feels so good, you will not care."

Gem frowned. "It isn't too bad." She rubbed the sore spot Cia had made.

"I can promise, my sister, you will be too busy having fun fucking to notice if it hurts."

"Mmm, I cannot wait to fuck with Og."

"Now that I have answered your questions, dear sister, it is time to return to the cave for the mid-day meal and to start the meal for the men when they return from hunting. They will be hungry and tired after the hunt." Cia flicked water off her slim, nude body with a smile for Gem. "I think tonight, Og will not be so 'busy.'"

"I hope you are right." Gem skimmed the water off her skin with her hands. "I am getting tired of waiting."

"Why are you frowning?"

"I must go with my father to another cave later tonight. He wants to show me to a man. What am I to do, Cia? I do not want to go."

Cia took Gem by the shoulders. "Do not worry. The man will want you, but your father will ask too much for you. The new man will not be willing to pay so much for you because he is a selfish man."

Gem sighed. "Are you sure?"

Cia rubbed her nose on Gem's. "Yes. I know many things. Your father is greedy, and he will ask too much. You will be home to the cave by tomorrow night."

"I am afraid. What if this man is willing to pay a lot for me?"

"Do not be afraid. There are many things I know but do not understand how I know. I just do. You will have to trust me, my sister. I do not lie to you."

Cia rubbed Gem's neck, gently easing the tightness. "Put on your beautiful dress, and we will return to the cave. No more worrying, my sister."

* * * *

Og crouched on his haunches, stroking his man-shaft as he spied on Gem and Cia in the pool. Gem was more perfect than the night sky, more lovely than a summer tree surrounded by flowers.

How he ached for her! His man-shaft swelled and throbbed with the rubbing of his hands. If only it were Gem's hands touching his shaft, or better yet, her mouth.

Many nights he sat by his dying fire and watched the young women enjoy each other's bodies. Their games were nothing unusual. At any given time of day in the busy cave, there would be couples enjoying each other. Life in a cave offered little or no privacy.

Og had a difficult time understanding why, with all the openness of the cave dwellers, he found Gem's body so fascinating. Why didn't his shaft come to life at the sight of Hoe or Cia's body? Cia was pretty and desirable, but her body did not excite him. Nor could he imagine taking her to be his mate.

Only Gem would do.

Gem flicked water at Cia and then off her slim form. Water flew, sending a shower of droplets all about. Og's shaft rose to a length and strength to rival the young saplings growing along the river bank. When the women dried each other with rabbit skins, his shaft throbbed with pleasure. He rubbed the head quickly, making his balls tighten. His whole body shuddered and his man-juice shot high in the air. Og bit his tongue , trying to stifle a moan.

Gem was going to be his. He had to have her for his own.

He crouched, watching the young women as they talked. For the first time in a long time, he wished they would talk with their hands. He could hear their voices but not what they were talking about. Could it be him or his friend Let?

Let was always whispering about Cia and how beautiful she was and how much he wanted to be her mate. Og had told him to get his spear sharpened and get busy, or he would not have enough skins to buy Cia from her father, especially if Cia was going to head of her own clan someday.

Og had seen Let working on his spear, so he must have taken Og's words to heart. The men had left the cave at the same time this rising, but Let had continued across the valley while Og held back to watch his soon-to-be mate.

Og looked about. Tec was getting higher in the sky. He had to hurry to make a kill so he would have something to show for his time away from the cave.

Stuffing his shaft back into the warmth of his hunting cover, Og picked up his spear and club and trotted across the valley, removing himself before the girls realized their bath had not been private. He ran as though the evil one was after him. Swift and sure, he traveled through the bushes and trees, avoiding the hunters from his cave. He galloped to a halt at a large fissure in the cliff wall surrounding the valley. By turning sideways, he was able to squeeze through and was soon loping across a second valley even larger than the one he left behind.

There were not many caves around this valley. He could count them on the fingers of one hand, which meant there weren't many hunters in this valley.

Today, he would find and kill the big antelope. He had seen it from afar many times. It was a beautiful, sleek, perfectly formed animal with massive horns. Even Tog would be impressed by the offering of the horns, for they would make deadly weapons.

After he tanned the antelope's skin, Og would approach Tog and ask for his daughter. Soon, the delicious Gem would be warming his bed every night. Her father was a greedy man, and he would not turn away the many skins Og had collected. The large antelope skin would be the final skin to be offered. Tog would not be able to resist. No man in the cave had ever offered so much for a woman.

Ah, Gem. What a fine mate she would make. How beautiful she would be draped naked over his bearskin with the firelight burnishing her body in flickering fire-light and her cloudy hair fanned out behind her head. Her legs would spread for him, and her cunt would weep for his shaft.

It would be wonderful to come home after a long, hard day of hunting to find his fire-pit glowing and Gem waiting for him with his evening meal. It was easy to picture her squatting in front of his fire, her skin flushed from the heat of cooking and her belly rounded with a child inside. She would look up to greet him, a soft, welcoming smile on her face.

She would open her legs to him every night, and when they slept, she would warm his body.

She would join him as he hunted. She would run beside him, her hair streaming behind her like mist. They would share his man-shaft in the open and drink and bathe in the clear streams rushing along the valley floor. Together, they would hunt and fish, and after Tec climbed the sky and settled for the night, they would sleep rolled up in his bearskin under one of the giant trees in the heart of the valley's forest.

To those who were observant, Gem had made her feelings for him plain, and his mother was not happy. She complained about the way Gem dressed, the fact she spoke openly to him and had been seen at his fire, raising her gaze to his. All these things had his mother angry and nervous.

Og grinned as he ran to the place he had last seen the antelope. His mother was jealous and followed the old ways. She would get over it. Gem was the woman he wanted, and he would have her. No matter what his mother or anyone did to change his mind.

He would cure and tan the last hide to perfection and make his offer to Tog.

Then, he would not be busy.

* * * *

The evening meal was finished. Gem and her mother were cleaning up when Cia appeared at their fire. She bowed and signed to Tog asking if Gem could join the younger people for a while.

Tog growled and signed, "Do not be late. I want to leave soon. I will be watching you."

Cia grabbed Gem's hand and they ran to join several of the young cave dwellers who were sitting around a fire at Tem's cave. Tem, like Og, was now old enough to be on his own. He, too, was searching for a woman to keep him warm at night and his cave clean during the day.

There were greetings spoken by everyone, and the noise level raised.

"Sit," Tem urged the women. "We are talking about many words tonight." They all had time to think. Hunting meant long days and short nights. And the women, too, had time to think as they worked around the fire-pit or scrapped skins clean.

"Tell us the words you have." Cia urged.

"Tem thinks a man's cock could be called a penis," Pat said quietly.

A young, handsome man stood , "I am Dik." He reached under his hunting skirt and pulled out his penis. "This is Dik, too. Do you like the word?" He shook his thick penis until the girls started to giggle. "Dik sounds like a good name."

"The word is a funny one. Dik, dik, dik," the young women chanted until the elders of the cave turned to stare hard at them.

There was a lot of giggling. The women put their hands over their mouths, but shaking shoulders gave them away.

They caught their breath and began again.

"Dik and penis. They are good words. We will use them," decided Cia.

Hoe frowned. "Who died and made you queen?"

Cia stared her sister down, eventually forcing Hoe to look away. "You know one day I will have my own clan. I do not want you in my clan. From now on you are not my sister."

Silence followed her words. Hoe stood and turned on the group. "One day you will all be sorry for the way you treated me." She turned to her sister. "Fuck you, Cia. I hope you die."

Cia laughed. "I will one day, but until then stay away from me and my friends. You are a bad woman."

Hoe stomped away, her bottom jiggling. The young men whistled and the women jeered until Hoe was out of sight.

"Now, start the speaking game, Lia. Do you have a new word?" Cia said.

Lia giggled. "I was thinking about mating. There must be a word to mean a man and woman will be one for life."

"Any idea?" Cia asked the group.

Lia wiggled her fingers. "I know the word 'merry' means happy."

"What if merry also meant to be forever one with each other?" Gem asked. "I think the woman will be 'wife.' Man will be 'husband' or 'lover.'"

Cia smiled. "I like those words." She looked at the group. "Do you like the words?"

They nodded.

"Any other words today?"

Chu stood. He patted his round, hard stomach. "I am 'chubby'?"

Everyone laughed.

Gem looked around and didn't see Og. He often joined the group, but tonight he wasn't there and she was hurting. Didn't he know she was about to be sold to another man?

Gem wished she had not turned her head because her father was signing for her to return, "Now."

Gem sighed. "I must go now. My father is taking me to another valley to sell me. I don't want to," she hesitated, "marry, any man but Og." Oh, no. She'd said it out loud. She covered her mouth and nodded her good-bye to her friends.

Cia squeezed her arm. "It will be all right, Gem. You will not be sold to another. We will see you in a few passings of Tec."

The moment Gem arrived at her father's fire, he wrapped a rough hand around her arm and tugged. "Hurry," he signed.

He signed to his mate they would return with two passings of Tec, but if it was longer, not to worry. He also promised to guard her only child. Nothing would happen to Gem. She was worth too much to lose or injure.

Her mother's eyes grew wet. "Be safe, my child," her mother signed.

"Yes, Mother," Gem signed.

"Be good. Do not make your father angry."

"No, Mother."

"Do not let him make you stay with a man you do not want."

"He will not listen."

"He will listen because he knows I will push him off the cliff if he does anything bad to my child."

"Tog," Ret signed, "do not harm Gem. You will regret it forever. I will make your life worth nothing."

"Yes, woman. I understand." He yanked on Gem's arm again, and she dug in her heels. She did not want to go with him.

Gem realized Og was back at his fire-pit staring at the wall. Something must have gone wrong today. It was obvious from the slope of his shoulders Og was brooding. His mother had not started his fire yet again, and there was no food roasting for him. He had to be starving. She should be taking care of him since his mother wouldn't.

"Now!" Her father was angry and his grip on her arm tightened.

She looked at Og and then at her father and decided if she didn't do as he wanted, her father would drag her by her heels. She was going to the other cave whether she wanted to or not. If she screamed, would Og save her?

Tog yanked harder, and Gem gave in. Og was ignoring her, and her father was hurting her. She might as well see what the new man was like. Maybe he wouldn't be so busy.

"Do not worry about Og," her mother signed. "I will make his fire and feed him. He will not suffer."

"Thank you, Mother." Gem wanted to tell her mother more, but before she could, Tog gave her arm a good, hard jerk, and she was out the wide opening of the cave. She stumbled as he pulled her down the path to the valley floor.

When she got her father's attention, she signed she would follow, and he finally let go of her arm and pushed her in front of him so she wouldn't disappear.

When they reached the end of the path, he pointed, and they headed across the valley to a cave far away from their home cave.

Tec was sinking behind the mountain, and it would be dark soon.

Gem carried a tar and grass covered club her father had stuck in the home fire-pit before they left the cave. It glowed, giving them a dim light to find their way. It was growing cool, and Gem shivered.

"Hurry, girl," her father signed. "I want to get as far as we can before we set up camp for the night. I told Heg we would be at his cave after the morning meal."

They walked for what seemed like half the night before Tog found a camping spot by a small stream. Gem looked back toward their home cave but couldn't see any light. They were too far away. Tec's sons had built their tiny fires in the dark above them. Those fires were the only thing she could see.

Tog waited impatiently for Gem to gather some small branches and dry grass. Her father was always so anxious it made Gem nervous. She could never please him. She next picked up some bigger branches and laid out the fire. First, she dug a hole as deep as her arm to the bend and as wide as her full arm. Then, she put in rocks to fill the bottom. Next, she laid out three pieces of coal and the grass, followed by the small branches and then the two thicker branches.

Tog grumbled and mumbled the whole time she worked. He held the torch so she could see what she was doing but otherwise didn't move to help. When the pit was laid out to his liking, he leaned forward and stuck the torch in and lit the grass. Before long there was a nice warmth surrounding them, and the plains didn't seem so frightening to Gem.

Gem scavenged more wood and laid it in a pile next to the pit. She would be responsible for keeping the fire going the rest of the night so her father could rest. He was a man and needed sleep. The meeting at the rising of Tec was an important one for Tog. Gem didn't care. She was not going to mate with any man other than Og. No matter how much her father pushed her.

Gem walked behind some large stones and made water, which she quickly covered with dirt so it wouldn't bring any night animals to the camp. Her father did the same, and when he returned, he tied a long piece of sinew around her ankle and his. He did not want her slipping away in the dark.

Tog held out his hand, and Gem rustled through the heavy sack she had been carrying. She pulled out a large piece of fur Ret had made by sewing small animal coats together and handed it to him. He wrapped the cover around his body, fur side in, and lay down close to the fire. Soon, he was snoring loudly.

Far off in the distance, an animal screamed, and Gem shivered and moved closer to the fire and prayed silently to Tec for her safety.

By the time Tec came over the top of the cliffs, Gem had the fire built back up and her father's morning drink brewing. It hadn't been easy to do without waking Tog since they were still tied together. She didn't want to wake him too soon since he was as grouchy as an old bear in the mornings.

Her mother had packed a sack of food for the trip, and Gem had made her father a morning meal. This time she ate while he slept so she didn't have to worry if there would be enough for her this day.

Tog woke, stretched, and untied the sinew. The moment she was loose, Gem ran behind the rock to relieve herself. It had been a long, uncomfortable night.

After Tog ate, Gem cleaned the camp and banked the fire. They would stay at the same place on their way back to their home. She took her time, which was not a good idea since her father was very anxious to get on the way and was in a bad temper.

Before she was ready, they were walking up the path to the cave where the new man waited and her father's friend, Heg, lived. Was it his son who wanted her for a mate? She had seen Heg. He was ugly, short, fat, hairy, and wrinkled. What would his son look like? She didn't want to think about it. Og was going to be her mate. No, he was going to be her husband.

At the opening of the cave, Tog stepped in and dropped his spear. He signed for all to see he was a friend and there to meet Heg. His friend came forward and gave him a bear hug so all knew Tog signed the truth.

Heg led Tog to his fire-pit, and Gem followed with her head down and her hands folded in front of her. She ached to stare around her and see if this cave was the same as the cave she came from. It probably was. It sounded the same as her home, but the smells were different.

The sound of crying babies echoed off the cave walls. Smoke from fires made her eyes burn, and the smell of bad meat made her belly tighten. At least her home did not smell of old smoke and bad food. At her cave, natural air shafts drew the smoke away, and the women were careful to not keep food more than a day or two.

Out of the corner of her eye, she spied several aged dwellers sitting at a fire-pit, wrapped in skins to stay warm. No matter what the weather outside, the caves were cool. Sometimes too cool, especially for the old, sick, or very young.

The two men signed for a long time. Without staring, Gem tried to watch without being caught. The men's fingers flew, and Gem only was able to understand a few words once in a while. From what she could figure out, Heg's son, Hot, was of age and ready to mate. He was tall, strong, and a good hunter.

Tog asked if Hot could make many children, and Heg smiled, showing short, brown, broken teeth. Gem shivered. Heg was nasty. All she could do was hope his son wouldn't be too terrible to look upon.

A shadow fell over Gem and cut her off from what little heat she'd been able to absorb from Heg's fire. Before she could stop herself, she raised her eyes and came face to face with a young man. Hot. It had to be Heg's son, Hot.

Gem sighed. Hot was almost as beautiful as Og. He was taller and darker with more body hair, sturdy, long legs, and a broad, muscular chest. His face was plucked clean of hair, and the dark, wavy hair of his head was clean and slicked back to show his face to advantage.

He had a firm jaw, a full-lipped mouth, close-set ears, and a fine nose. He was easy to look upon. His lips twitched. He was trying not to smile. Gem couldn't help but compare his body to Og's, and the two men were similar in many ways except for the color of their hair and the size of their cocks.

Hot wore a short, tanned hunting cover which wasn't long enough to cover his large, dark cock. It was a fine cock, so large she doubted she could wrap one hand around it, much less suck on him. The skin hood protecting the knob of his cock was closed, but as she stared, the head of his cock came into view and a pearl of man-juice formed on the end.

Hot seemed to like her.

Gem folded her arms and frowned. She did not care how lovely his cock was. He was not going to be her mate.

Hot knelt down in front of her and tipped her face up so he could look at her. His cock dangled, just missing brushing in the dirt. Oh, he was very large. Perhaps she had decided too soon not to mate with anyone besides Og.

Hot stood and signed to her father, "She is pretty. Does she speak?"

Tog shrugged and signed, "She speaks, and she signs. She cooks and keeps a clean cave. She is a good hunter and can build a fire in the blink of an eye. She is a good girl and will make a good mate."

Hot looked at her. "Open your covering, girl," he signed.

Gem shook her head.

Tog grabbed her arm. "Do what he asks, girl, or I will beat you."

Hot shook his head. "No beating." He stepped close to Gem, and she stepped back. He was too close and much too large. He took the front of her dress in his hands and pulled it open, revealing her naked body. Gem tried to cover herself, but he gently tugged her hands away and held on to them.

Hot smiled. "She is good. I will taste her."

Tog put a hand on Hot's arm. "Not before we bargain. She is untried and will stay that way until I get a good price for her."

Hot covered Gem's body with her garment and stroked her arm. "Nice."

The three men sat around Heg's fire-pit, and Heg poured out bowls of fermented roots called potatoes. Gem had tasted it once or twice, and it was strong and made her head feel funny.

Gem slipped into the shadows and tried to watch all the flying fingers. So far it looked as if her father was not happy with the offer Hot had made of a mammoth skin and a tiger skin.

Tog unrolled the mammoth skin and laid it on the floor. He frowned when he noticed several tears and matted fur. The tiger skin was even in worse shape.

Gem put a hand over her mouth to cover her smile. Thank Tec her father thought she was worth a lot more than two ratty skins.

Hot disappeared into his sleeping cave and returned with a large antelope skin. He unrolled it, but again Tog frowned and shook his head.

Hot's face grew dark, and Gem slipped farther into the shadows. She checked to see how close she was to the cave opening in case she had to run. Friends or not, it looked like the three men were about to start bashing each other with their clubs.

Heg put a hand on Tog's arm. "We are friends. We will not let my son cause us to fight."

Tog put his hand over his friend's. "Good. I do not want to fight, but I will not give my daughter away for nothing. She is worth much more than these paltry skins."

"It might be better if you went on your way, Tog. I will speak with Hot, and if he makes some better captures, he will come to your cave to ask for Gem as a mate."

Tog stood, signed his thanks for the drink, grabbed Gem from her hiding place, and yanked her out of the cave. He mumbled and grumbled all the way to their campsite. He set a rapid pace, and Gem was glad more than once she had long legs or she would have been left behind by now.

It was still light when the campsite came into view. Gem sighed. They were halfway home. She was anxious to see Og. She needed to reassure herself he was as beautiful as she remembered.

Hot would have been a good mate to sleep with and fuck, but she had a feeling he was lazy and wouldn't be a good provider. If he couldn't tan skins well, he also couldn't hunt well. His hunting skills showed in the damage to the skins he'd tried to use to buy her.

Tog refused to sign with her. He was angry he hadn't been able to sell her. Even if her mother would be happy, it would take Tog a few passings of Tec before he would forgive her for not being bought.

* * * *

It was good to be back at the home-fire. Her mother had greeted them with signings of joy and love. Even Tog had been given a bear hug, which turned his face dark red. Gem giggled. Her father liked being hugged by her mother whether he wanted to admit it or not.

Ret had the evening meal simmering, and soon Tog was settled by the fire with a bowl warm in his hands. While he ate, Gem and her mother slipped into the shadows and signed. Ret tried not to laugh when Gem told her about Hot's large cock and how he showed himself.

Ret asked if Gem liked him and didn't seem surprised when Gem signed her dislike of the man.

Gem accepted a bowl of hot liquid to sip, and her mother continued to sign many questions about the journey. Gem tried to watch her mother's hands and search the cave at the same time. She could not find Og.

"Mother," Gem interrupted, signing, "where is Og?"

Ret shrugged. "I do not know. I saw Hoe go to his fire and open her skirt for him." Ret kept her head down. Gem wanted to see what was in her eyes, but her mother hid her face.

"Did he touch her?" Gem's voice quivered. She bit her lip to keep from crying.

Ret nodded. "He ran his hands over her ass and up her legs. He stood, and she rubbed her teats against his chest."

Gem began to weep. No wonder he was too busy for her.

Ret grabbed Gem's hand. "To be honest, Gem, he seemed angry and did not go any further to pleasure Hoe. She put her mouth on his, and Og pushed her away."

"That is good, isn't it Mother?"

"Probably. I don't think his cock was hard. I couldn't see the front of his hunting skirt lift. You need to know Hoe tried very hard to interest Og. She laid on his bed and opened her legs. She squeezed her tits and moaned, but Og ignored her. He packed a sack and went out late in the dark the night you and your father left and has not yet returned. His mother is getting worried."

"I will go find him."

"No. You will not leave. He took his spear, club, and sack. I am sure he will be fine, and I'm sure he will return soon." She patted

Gem's leg. "Do not worry. Og is brave and strong. He wants you for his mate. He will be back before Tec sets tomorrow."

"You know this as truth, Mother? He wants me?"

"I've seen him watch you when you are not looking. Yes, he wants you for a mate, and he will not wait much longer before asking to buy you from your father."

"Do you approve, Mother?"

Ret smiled and nodded. "He is very beautiful, strong, well-built, works hard, and wants you. It will not be long."

Tog growled and signed, "Stop signing. You are annoying me."

The women smiled at each other and moved farther into the dark. Gem couldn't control her anxiety. She wanted him. She'd wanted Og for a long time. "Mother, are you sure he did not fuck Hoe?"

"I'm sure. I watched closely. Hoe is not a nice girl. She steals men from their mates. I saw Og pack and leave before Hoe could get him down on the bear rug. On his way out the door, he stopped and signed to me he would return because he was going to buy you."

Gem was so happy she wanted to sing. Perhaps Lia would lead them in a song of jubilation tonight. Gem wanted to tell the world soon Og would be her lover, her husband.

"I can't believe he stopped to talk to you, Mother. Did he say anything else?"

"No, my daughter. Just that you were his. What had happened with Hoe was none of his doing." Her mother patted Gem's knee. "Now, be silent and stay still so your father can eat."

When Tog was through with his meal, the women ate their meal and cleared away the remnants. Soon, all were curled in their bearskin rugs. Tog snored loudly, and Gem wiggled around trying to find a comfortable spot. Where was Og? She should be with him tonight. The trip to visit Heg and Hot had been a waste of precious time.

With Hoe to entertain him, she was surprised he'd had time to stop at her home and speak to her mother. Perhaps he did care. The fact he'd talked to her mother gave her hope.

Gem wondered it mattered to Og because her father had taken her to sell. Since he was always busy, she was surprised Og had stopped to speak to her mother. Even though he acted as if he didn't care, Og had noticed she was gone.

At last Tec's light began to creep into the main cave, and Gem rose and cooked the morning meal. After the family ate, Tog grabbed his spear and left, but not before grunting and rubbing his nose on Ret's.

Ret went out to dig up food hidden in the cold dirt while Gem spruced up their part of the cave.

Later, she and Cia spent time sitting on the ledge outside the cave, talking about Gem's visit with Hot and Heg.

Cia was impressed with the size of Hot's cock and asked many questions about his male parts. Gem described Hot as best she could using some of the new words and what signs were available.

The young women laughed and giggled. Gem admitted Hot was very handsome. She and Hot would have made large, strong babies, but she wanted Og to be the father of her children. His children would be even larger, stronger and smart.

Cia nodded. "Og is beautiful, and he is a good hunter. He will keep you warm at night and bring home much food to keep you and your children fed. He is a good man and...he also has a handsome cock. I think he will keep you happy for many seasons."

"If I do not get a chance soon to tempt him into my bed, I will never find out. Where has he gone?"

"Has he been gone a long time, my sister?"

"My mother said he left right after father and I did." She counted her fingers. "A long time."

Cia nodded. "He has been gone since you left with your father. He took his spear and club."

"What was he wearing?"

"His hunting skirt and he carried a pack on his back." Cia grinned. "He followed you for a long way. I watched. I think he followed you the whole way, and when he was sure you were safe, he went hunting."

"I hope he is safe."

Cia laughed. "Look across the valley, my sister. Your wish has come true, for he is heading our way as we speak."

* * * *

Cia was right. It was Og.

The day was drawing to a close. Gem stood and leaned against the chilly rocks at the cave's opening. She didn't realize her friend had left her. Gem was intent on watching Og. She stared hard across the valley. Every day the land began to awaken to the warmth of Tec.

Green buds on slender limbs wave in the afternoon breeze and the air crisped as the day ended

Gem's breath wisped around her like a cloud of steam. She was so cold her teats had tightened into hard knots, the perfect size for a man to suck on, and her dress clung to them like a second skin. Warm and yet not warm enough. She should have gathered up her fur cape earlier.

But now, it was too late. She could not take her eyes off of Og. He trotted easily along the tree line before turning to head straight toward the cave.

Her whole body leaned forward to give her a better view of the man she wanted. He was so strong and manly. His long stride brought him closer by the moment.

His trip had been successful because over his broad shoulders rested the tan-furred body of a massive animal. Its huge horns nearly touched the ground. How could he carry something so large and not injure himself?

Og moved with steady grace. He held his body straight, carrying the beast as though it weighed no more than a rabbit. Tec, peeking over the edge of the mountains, shot streaks of gold across Og's body.

Gem sighed. Og was so large and manly.

"He is beautiful," Cia whispered in Gem's ear.

Gem jumped. "Where have you been?"

"Checking on the evening meal. Do you want me to bring you a warm cover?"

"No. Watching him keeps me warm. Soon, he will be mine."

"I thought you worried he would always be too busy for you," her friend teased.

Pushing aside the fur covering her titties, Gem turned to Cia. "I will show him these. Once he sees them, how can he not want me?"

Hoe, Cia's sister, walked out of the cave and glared at Gem. "Og wants me, not you. All know his mother intends for him to take a mate, and it will not be you. Ke does not like you. She likes me."

Cia cupped a gentle hand on Gem's teat. "I think Gem's teats are beautiful. I love the way the nipples tighten when I suck them." She turned her ire on Hoe. "You are lying, Hoe. Gem's mother saw him turn you away. Ke does not want you for her son. Ke has said many times no woman will do and that means you, too."

"Nipples?" Gem asked, trying to ignore Hoe.

Cia flicked the dark pink tip of her teat. "Yes, I have named these 'nipples.' Do you like the word?"

"I do not. We have enough words," Hoe said. "Ke does not think women should waste time playing with words."

Gem and Cia growled at Hoe, and she disappeared as rapidly as she had appeared.

"Ignore her, Gem. Hoe is jealous of you because she knows Og desires you and turned her away. She is angry."

Gem sighed. "I hope you are right."

Cia laughed and tweaked Gem's nipple. "I am right. You will see. Do you like when I do this?"

"Yes, I like it. I also like when you suckle them, my sister-friend."

Cia touched her again. "Just imagine how nice it will feel when Og touches you there with *his* mouth and nips you with his teeth."

"Ooh, I cannot wait much longer, sister."

Gem checked Og's progress across the valley floor. He had nearly finished climbing the rocky slope up to the cave. Sometime during the day, he had taken off his hunting vest, and his broad chest showed signs of blood.

Gem's heart dipped. Had he been injured? But his stride was full of energy, and no pain lined his face. The blood must be from the animal draped around him.

Og strode toward her, giving Gem time to admire the shape of his hard body. She watched the muscles in his legs flex with each step. His arms bulged from the weight of the animal over his shoulders. Soon, he was close enough she could see Og's massive cock pushing against his hunting wrap.

Tonight she would touch his penis. Suckle him until he gave her his baby-making juice.

Cia had taught her many things a woman could do to a man to please him without taking his cock inside her body. She had waited long enough. She would wait no longer for the taste and feel of Og.

Sweat rolled down Og's forehead and cheeks and dropped to his bare, glistening upper body. The male nipples nearly hidden in his chest hair glittered and begged to be licked and nipped.

"Og!" Hoe called, but he did not turn to her.

Where had Hoe come from? Gem thought she had gone away. It pleased her that Og was ignoring Hoe.

But Gem was still angry when she thought about Og touching Hoe's body. Stop, she warned herself, Og had turned Hoe away at the last moment. At least that's what her mother said. Perhaps her mother was not telling her everything.

He could have taken Hoe to his bed when her mother was not looking. Or Hoe might have gone with Og on the beginning of his trip, ridden his cock, then returned to the cave.

Before Gem could make herself angrier, Og came to a halt in front of Gem and stared until she had to meet his gaze. When he had her attention, he dropped the massive body of the antelope at her feet.

"I will need help tonight," Og declared. "My mother will not help me."

"I will help you," Hoe said.

"I will think about it." He paused, and Gem ground her teeth to keep from hitting either him or Hoe.

"I have decided, Hoe. I do not want your help. Go away. I want Gem to help me." Og crossed his arms. "Tonight."

Hoe kicked out at Gem, turned, and ran back into the cave.

He wanted her, Gem, tonight? Was this a dream? A vision? Was he real? Gem reached out a finger. He was real. Wet with sweat and blood, he was so totally male, and for the first time, his maleness frightened her.

Her fear passed as quickly as it struck. "I will help you, Og," she whispered.

"Good. After the evening meal, I will meet you outside by the fire to ready this beast."

Her heart fluttering, she said, "I will join you as soon as my father is done eating."

He nodded his approval. "Do not forget to wear your work apron."

She bowed her head, and trembling with excitement, she rushed past Cia and Og to her home fire. A short time later, Og entered the cave and strode past her. Gem watched him. It was not her fault he had such a nice, tight bottom.

She sighed. No one had tended Og's fire. She could only see a tiny glow. Og's mother had made it clear to the women of the cave it was time Og chose a mate. Ke often signed to others that she would no longer keep his fire going or cook his meals. He needed a mate. Ke told the others she was tired of waiting on Og.

Gem watched Og push small bits of wood into the glow and wait patiently for it to flare before adding more wood and a piece of coal.

Soon, he had a good fire going. He might be warm, but there was nothing to eat.

His mother was making it clear she was done helping him. Gem was tempted to offer him food, but since he had not approached her father yet, she could not bring him to their fire for food. Her mother would not mind, but her father would explode like a bad piece of coal.

Gem watched Og search for food to eat as she prepared the meal for her father. While Og's meal cooked, he disappeared into his sleeping cave, and soon he returned carrying his work apron. The garment was stiff with blood from many animals, dirty. His mother had not washed it for him in many moons. The rough skin rubbing against his body had to hurt. Especially his long, semi-hard cock.

Another message to Og from his mother.

Gem felt bad for Og. She would have cleaned his covering and softened it so he could work in comfort. His mother was being mean, and Og didn't deserve such bad treatment. She would treat him well, tending to his bed, his body, his fire, and his children. She would make him a happy man.

Gem could not understand why Og's mother did not like her. She was hard working, and one day she would be the clan's medicine woman. Neither her mother nor Cia's understood why Ke did not approve of Gem. Maybe Gem was too smart, and it frightened Ke.

"Father?" Gem approached Tog with respectful subservience.

"Yes, daughter," he signed before taking a huge bite of roasted rabbit chewing vigorously.

"I would help Og tonight."

"Oh?"

She did not like the way his fingers snapped, but she continued. "He has asked me to help him dress out an antelope. It is very large, and he needs help."

"I have seen the animal. He left it for all to see as they walked into the cave." Forehead wrinkled in thought, Tog took another bite of rabbit. "I suppose you may help him, girl."

"Thank you," Gem signed. She was careful to keep her eyes firmly staring at the ground.

Her father poked her and signed, "Where is your mother, girl?"

"I think she is helping Moi give birth."

"I am in need of relief. Get me Hoe," he demanded, rubbing his cock.

Gem pretended not to read his signs. "Did you have a good day hunting?"

Tog held out his bowl for more rabbit. "Not as good as Og but good enough."

Finally, Gem had the eating area cleared. She slipped out of her woven dress, folded it, and laid it on her sleeping skin. Taking up her work apron, she fastened it at her back and walked to the main opening of the cave. Back straight, teats pointing high, hair tied on top of her head with a leather strap, she strode past several fires, drawing much attention as she went.

"Where are you going, Gem?" Young Rat, a child of five summers, signed curiously.

"I am going to help Og."

Rat laughed. "I saw his catch. It is very big." The child held his hands far apart.

Gem nodded and laughed with the small boy. "Yes, it is. That is why he needs help."

"I will watch," the child signed.

His mother grabbed his arm. "No. It is time to sleep." She pushed Rat toward the sleeping cave and sent Gem a knowing wink. "Have a good time, sister."

"I will." Gem ran her shaking hands down her hips and over the smooth leather apron. Tonight, she would be nearly naked, working side by side with Og. He, too, would be nearly naked. It was going to be a trial to keep from touching his wonderful, hard, golden-haired body.

It would be harder still to ignore his cock. His lovely, large shaft.

Busy

At the entrance to the cave, Og stood next to the antelope, broad hands on his slim hips. With his legs spread for balance, he rocked back and forth on the balls of his feet. "Good. You are here. Come. We have much work to do."

Gem sighed at the beauty of the man she wanted for her mate. His work apron barely concealed his muscular behind, and in the front, it just covered his manhood.

It was going to be a long night. She would never be able to keep her hands off his penis.

Overhead, the night sky was bright with the twinkle of faraway fires, signal lights built by Tec's sons every night to light the way. The moon, Poc, had risen over the top of the cliffs.

"It is cold. I have built a fire to work by," Og said, bending to take the head of the antelope in his hands. "It is by the big stone."

Gem stared at the globes of Og's firm bottom and put out a trembling hand. Her fingers were within inches of touching him when Og said, "Take the hind legs, girl, and we will move the animal to the light."

Gem yanked her hand back and hurried to do as he directed, but the animal was stiff and heavy in death, and she was afraid she wouldn't be of much help moving the carcass. The big stone, where many of their clan prepared their animals, was at the foot of the cliff, near a hot springs that emptied into a fast-moving stream for cleaning. Finally, she managed a firm grasp on the beast. Lifting, using her knees for balance, Gem began to help Og move the animal.

"Take care," Og warned her as they walked beyond the cave to the big stone and the fire.

He'd spread an old tanned skin close, but not too close, to the fire-pit. They lay the carcass on the skin, taking care not to damage the horns. Og squatted and picked up an obsidian knife he had made. Taking one horn in his large hand, he sliced it free of the animal's head and handed it to Gem. Soon, both horns lay safely out of the way.

"I will clean them later," Og said. While Gem watched, he eviscerated the carcass and piled the entrails on another skin. They would also be washed and used for string or casings. No part of the animal would be wasted. He handed Gem a smaller obsidian knife, and at his direction, they began to skin the antelope.

Hours later, they sat side by side at the edge of the hot pool. Close enough their bodies warmed one another in the cool night air, but not so close that they touched. Too exhausted to move, covered in blood and filth, Gem couldn't wait to ease into the soothing waters of the heated pool. Would Og join her? He'd spent the whole evening trying not to stare at her titties and had done a poor job of it.

Gem had to smile when she thought about his long, hard cock peeking from under his work apron, making it clear he hungered for her. More than once, she'd noticed a drop of man-juice on his tip. His cock's protective hood was nowhere in sight, the dark knob fully exposed. Yes, he hungered for her as she hungered for him tonight.

Gem had gone out of her way to rub her nipples against his arm or back more than once. Each time, his cock had grown longer and firmer. She'd also made sure to spread her thighs, giving him a good, clear view of her cunt and the honey which trickled hotly from her.

He had to be the cave's idiot not to have noticed how much she wanted him.

"Og?"

"Yes?"

"We should clean our bodies."

He nodded. "Yes, but I think I am busy."

She smiled. "No. You are not busy."

He grinned. "I think I am...busy."

Gem stood, untied her work apron, and let it drop to the cold, hard ground. "I do not think so."

Og lifted his gaze and stared openly at her in the light of the moon. The night air was chill, but she was hot inside. She laughed softly when he swallowed. "You are not busy, Og."

His eyes never strayed from the curls protecting her cunt. Feeling confident, Gem shifted and parted her legs, widening her stance.

Og stood as though in a trance and unfastened his work apron. It dropped to the ground with a loud thump. His massive cock sprang into view.

Gem nearly sobbed with longing. Instead, she managed to stammer, "O–Og?"

He gave her a knowing look and nodded. "Yes?"

"I will touch you."

He laughed and touched himself instead, lifting and cupping his cock and balls before letting them free. They bobbed and rolled against his thighs. His cock pointed straight at her.

"I am busy," he said.

His boy-child grin told Gem he was teasing, so she stuck out a trembling hand and touched the very tip of his exposed cock. A pearly drop of his seed appeared, and Gem licked her lips. "I will taste you now," she said. She was not asking permission.

His hips bucked as though something had hit him from behind. "I think I am busy."

Gem stamped her foot. "You are not."

Og cupped his cock and balls, offering them up to her like a gift to the gods. "I am busy, girl."

Gem's heart tipped, and her eyes filled with tears. He didn't want her.

"I am busy with you," Og continued in his deep, rough voice, sending her heart spiraling out of control.

"Oh!" She was so excited and happy she could barely breathe.

Og moved a step closer and she, suddenly unsure what to do, took a step backward. Her foot slipped on the wet rocks, and she threw her hands up in surprise. Before she could stop, she fell, landing in the pond with a great splash, and sank like a stone to the bottom.

Gem wanted to die. How could this have happened right in front of Og? Right before she got to taste his beautiful cock? He would probably leave her now since she'd made a fool of herself.

Kicking hard, she rose to the surface and came face to face with her almost-lover. When had he slid into the water? Before she could protest, she was in his arms and he was nuzzling her neck.

He gently turned her and slid his strong arms around her ribcage. Her back was against the solid wall of his chest, his cock long and hard between her bottom and his hips. The warm water surrounded them like an extra embrace while mist rose from the surface, hiding them in their own little world.

The touch of his heated cock against her skin turned her legs soft and wobbly as a toddling baby. She was weaker than a newborn tiger cub.

She whimpered when his hands cupped her titties. His fingers pinched and tweaked at her nipples until she was writhing and crying his name. He nipped at her tender neck, sucking and licking.

Eager to give him everything, Gem turned in his arms and arched her back, bringing her nipples close to his mouth. Og took advantage of the shift of her position to dip his head and begin sucking.

"Ahhh," she moaned, throwing her head back. Her moan echoed through the valley, ricocheting off the rocks surrounding them. "More, Og, more. Do it harder. Suck harder. Oh, it feels so good."

Og lifted his mouth from her nipple and whispered harshly, "Silent. No one must hear us."

Gem clamped her lips tightly together and pulled his head back toward her titties. "More."

He eagerly latched on to a nipple, sucking it into his heated, wet mouth. He twirled his tongue around her nipple, and Gem bit the inside of her mouth so she wouldn't scream.

"Yes," Gem groaned, "yes. More."

Og lifted his head again. "Put your legs around me, girl."

Gem wrapped her legs around his body and rocked her cunt against his belly. His rampant cock nudged her bottom, seeking entry to her open cunt. Gem rocked against him, moaning like a wounded animal. She had waited so long to touch and be touched by him. She was frantic with need. Her wet body slipped closer to his cock. The tip touched the edges of her cunt, and she began to whimper softly.

"Gem, girl. Where are you?"

Oh, Tec! Her father was calling from the cave entrance. Soon, he would come searching for her. How long had she and Og been gone? Longer than she should have been or her father wouldn't be searching for her.

Gem pushed against Og's broad, lightly furred shoulders. "Put me down. My father is calling me. He will find us soon."

"So?" Og laughed quietly and nuzzled her swollen nipple. "What does it matter?"

"He will be very angry. He is saving me for the highest offer."

"I will take you now. You are mine, Gem." Og wasn't to be deterred. His cock was sweeping between the cheeks of her bottom and would soon gain entry to her cunt. The water lapped at her body, spreading its warmth to her insides. She was ready for Og to put his cock into her. So ready, her whole body trembled in his arms. All the advice Cia had given her about what men and women could do together besides put his cock inside her made her head spin. . She wanted him.

Now!

The lips of her cunt opened wider at his touch. "Yes," she whispered when his cock brushed against her swollen nub, the one she and Cia had named "clit." The shock of his touch brought another scream to her lips.

"Gem! Are you hurt?" Tog's loud call told them he was very close. "You should be done helping Og by now, girl."

Og let out a quiet groan that sounded as if he was in pain. "You are right, Gem. He will be angry."

He pushed at her legs, loosening her grip, and pried her hands from his shoulders. He wiped her face and urged her with hand signals to drift away. Silently, he dove and swam underwater until he was nowhere in sight. Like an otter, he was gone. If he slipped out of the pool, Gem didn't hear it.

Tog stood at the edge of the pool. Steam swirled and curled around his stocky, imposing figure. "Are you hurt, girl?"

Gem shook her head. "No, Father. I stepped on something sharp. I am sorry I made you leave the cave at night."

"Get out of the pool. It is time you were in the sleeping cave. Your mother is worried."

Shaking all over, Gem did as he ordered, hoping Tog would not notice her swollen nipples and flushed skin.

Under her father's stern eye, she picked up her work apron and trotted back to the cave.

Tog, too dignified to run, hitched up his covering, which immediately slid back down under his belly as he slowly made his way back to his fire-pit.

By the time he walked into the sleeping area, Gem was curled up in her bear skin with her eyes closed.

Hoe was waiting for him in his sleeping rug. Ret was probably still trying to deliver the baby. There had been a lot of screaming echoing through the cave all day, so the birthing was not going well, but it didn't mean anything to Tog.

Soon, he and Hoe were grunting and making a lot of noise.

Gem pretended to be asleep. Instead of listening to Hoe relieve her father, she wished she could be with Og on his sleeping pallet, sharing his penis. Would Tog never finish?

Finally, it quieted, and Tog started snoring.

Gem watched Hoe leave and sighed with relief. Eventually, the baby would be born, and Ret would be home. Ret had little or no love or kind feelings for Hoe, and if she found Hoe in bed with Tog, there might be a loud argument.

Gem watched Hoe head toward her own cave and was pleased. Suddenly, Hoe changed directions and headed to Og's fire. No. She wouldn't. Hoe clambered under the bear skin with Og, and Gem began to cry. Gem turned her face to the wall. She couldn't bear to know Hoe was going to receive the pleasure Gem had wanted. Hoe would benefit from the excitement Gem had raised his penis and body to.

Gem lay awake long into the night thinking about Og and Hoe. How she wanted to climb out of her bearskin and run to Og's. She longed to kick Hoe, hit her with a rock. But hurting Hoe could get Gem banished from the clan and then she would never have Og. Hoe, if she lived, would be the winner.

Og was Gem's. She had waited a whole lifetime for him. She would not do anything to lose him now because of a stupid woman.

Og had been so wonderful tonight. Surely, he was going to make an offer for her. Tog expected a lot from any man willing to buy her. Would Og have enough? Already, several men had made offers of two or three fine skins, but Tog had turned them down. She had not protested. No man but Og would do.

What did Og have besides the antelope? Surely, he had not given everything he killed to his mother.

Did he even plan to offer for Gem? The way Og had been at the pond tonight, he seemed to be pleased with her body.

It wasn't a dream. He had said, "You are mine, Gem."

Gem did not want to wait any longer to find out whether Og would offer for her, but she dare not defy her father. Tog was like Ke. Old fashioned. Her father had certain ideas about finding a mate, and a woman picking her own was forbidden as far as Tog was concerned. The old ways were the best ways, Tog had said many times.

She hoped she did not grow old waiting for Og.

She also hoped and prayed to Tec that Hoe had not stayed with Og, but she was afraid to turn from the wall for fear of what she would see.

* * * *

Many days passed. Gem had almost given up hope Og would make an offer for her. Every time she stopped by his fire, he told her he was busy.

The only good thing in her life was the fact Cia had seen Og kick Hoe out of his bed the night Gem could not bring herself to look.

Tec walked across the sky many times, and Gem stopped crying herself to sleep. She simply did not sleep at all. Instead, she lay awake thinking about Og's cock and how lovely it had felt rubbing her clit. Much, much better than when Cia rubbed it for her. How would his cock feel inside her cunt? Her body cried for him, and she touched herself or played with Cia, but it was not enough.

It had taken two passings of Tec before her mother came back from bringing the new baby into the cave family. The mother had been torn but would heal if her friends and mother helped her for a few days. Ke continued to push Og to find a wife. She told everyone who would watch her fingers it would not be Gem and it would not be Hoe. She would find someone special for her perfect son.

And every time Gem tried to speak to him, Og said he was busy.

When she overheard Hoe bragging Og was nearly hers, Gem realized she could wait no longer. Desperate for Og's attention, Gem put on her prettiest dress, made of the finest yarns her mother had woven. It was so fine one could see right through it, finer than the spider webs hanging in the corners of the cave.

Gem looked down at her body and was pleased with what she saw. Her nipples stood out like ripe berries. Her woman curls, light as they were, showed through the weave. There was nothing coy about her covering. Everything was there for Og to see. And if the dress didn't work, she planned to bare her cunt and weep on his cave floor.

* * * *

When Og returned from hunting, Gem squatted at his fire. For the first time in many passings of Tec, his home was warm, bright, clean and welcoming. It was nice to be home. So different from the many nights his mother had ignored his coals.

Gem smiled a welcome. "Greetings, warrior. Your night meal is not quite done. You have time to jump in the pool for a soothing swim."

Og looked down on her and imagined she was his mate already. Hunger rose in him, and when her eyes drifted down the front of his hunting cover, his cock stirred.

Gem blushed.

"A swim…yes. I will swim." The big antelope hide was not quite ready. Or was it? He had not checked it today. "Will you be gone when I return?"

She gave him a delighted grin. "No. I will stay, clean up after your meal, and give you a massage to ease your aching body."

He nodded and strode into his sleeping cave to gather his cleansing scrub. Just as she had promised, she was still by his fire when he returned from the pool. In the flickering orange light, she was more beautiful than the night sky or the flowers blossoming in the spring. The fabric of her covering flowed about her, moving like the breeze that tickled the grain in the summer. The covering was so thin, he could see her wonderful body beneath. Her cloud-bright hair swept past her shoulders, curling forward so he could not see her eyes.

"Gem?" he said.

She shook her hair back and smiled. Og's cock jumped and twitched anxiously under his leather apron. "Go home, girl."

Her beautiful smile turned to a frown. "No."

"Yes. Go . I am busy."

"You are not busy. I will not go home."

"I am busy," he insisted, taking the bowl she offered him. He sat with his back to her and began to eat. "Go home. I will talk to your father."

"When?" she demanded.

"I will do it later. Go home, girl."

"Please let me stay. I will give you a massage. We will mate."

He didn't want Gem to see how she was affecting him, so he kept his back to her and continued to eat. "Go home. I will come very soon."

"No."

He had no idea sweet, soft Gem could be so determined. His mother had been right. Gem did not follow the old ways of waiting for a man to come to her. Og sighed. Despite her stubbornness, or because of it, he wanted her with all his body. He did not want to tell her his plans, but if she continued to stay at his fire, she was going to spoil everything.

"Go home now, girl, and I will speak to your father this night." He paused and took a deep breath. "Then, if he agrees, we will mate."

"But—"

"Go now or your father will not agree. We will not anger your father."

Gem broke into a sob, and Og felt like the dogs lurking in the shadows of the cave. He softened his voice and turned to her. "Trust me, Gem. I will be there soon."

Gem swiped at her eyes and finally seemed to understand. "You will come, tonight?"

He nodded. "Yes."

"Soon?"

"Yes."

"We will mate?"

"Oh, yes. We will mate. Many, many times."

Her face grew flushed. "Many times?"

"More than you ever dreamed," he assured her with a wicked grin.

"Oh."

"Are you frightened, girl?"

She shook her head.

"Good, do not be. I have waited many years for you, Soon you will be mine. I will not hurt you. Only give you many pleasures."

It was with great relief Og watched Gem slip away to her father's fire. How he wished he could take her now, but if he did, her father would never give her to him. Tonight, he would make his offer, an offer even Tog would not be able to resist.

Og took a good deal of time to ready himself for his evening at Tog's fire. He smoothed all the light golden hair on his body and head. Using a tiny clam shell and a large piece of mica as a mirror, he plucked the stray hairs from his face, ensuring it was as smooth as a newborn baby's bottom.

When he finished grooming, Og tied on his finest apron. He had made the apron especially for tonight. After pounding the leather until it was as thin as a leaf, he'd cut the leather so it fit perfectly and showed his hunter's body to the best advantage. He'd been careful to be sure the leather covered his cock so Tog would not be offended by his strength and size. In no way did he want to offend Tog.

And the antelope skin was ready.

He bent to pick up the pile of skins and realized he had a large problem. The skins were so many, he couldn't carry them all at one time. He called to his friend Let and begged for his help. Let knew what Og was about to do and gave him a hard time, but eventually Let picked up half the skins and they made their way to Tog's fire.

The main cave was silent but full of energy as the dwellers watched the two men walk quietly to Tog's cave.

Not even a baby cried.

This was the biggest bride's price the cave dwellers had ever seen.

Og stopped and took a deep breath. "Let, my brother-friend, I would ask a favor of you tonight."

"Yes?"

"Please do not speak or sign unless I ask you to. This is between Tog and me."

Let nodded. "I understand."

The men continued on their way, arms loaded down with booty.

At the edge of his sleeping cave, Tog stood, arms folded, heavy legs akimbo, and a deep frown on his face.

"May we join you, Tog?" Og asked gesturing toward Let.

"You may both join me. Come and sit." Tog held out a hand.

Let and Og piled the skins at Tog's feet. Og folded his long legs and sank down in front of the fire. Gem stood in the doorway to the sleeping cave, a terrified look on her beautiful face. Ret stood next to her daughter, smiling.

"Well," Tog demanded.

Og took a deep, relaxing breath. "I have come to offer for your daughter. I would take her as my mate."

Tog coughed and spat onto the floor. "She is untried, and she will be medicine woman one day. You cannot afford her, boy."

"I would give you much for her hand," Og said softly.

"Show me, and I will decide."

Og didn't understand Tog's attitude. Tog didn't want to keep his daughter any longer, yet he expected whoever offered for her to give so much for her hand. Of course, Gem was worth whatever her father demanded. She was also worth putting up with the blustering display.

Og spread a finely striped tiger skin. "It is unblemished, and the claws are all there," Og assured the older man.

Tog scowled. He did not look impressed.

Gem and her mother smiled, giving Og courage to continue.

Og spread an even larger spotted skin and was relieved to see Tog's eyes light up. Greedy pig. This skin, too, was flawless. Next, Og proceeded to open and spread four antelope skins, tanned to perfection. Tog leaned forward, his eyes alight with a hunger to have it all.

Last, Og unrolled the new antelope skin. It was so large, Let had to help him spread it fully. It was the finest, softest skin Og had ever tanned. There were no flaws. It was large enough to make a fine suit of clothing for Gem's father, or a warm blanket for the winter cold, or even a rug for the whole floor.

Though drool had gathered in the corner of his mouth like a starving dog, Tog pretended to be unimpressed. "That is all?" he asked.

Behind him, Og heard Gem gasp, and he was tempted to hit the short, stocky man. Instead, he took the two superb antelope horns from Let and held them out.

"These are also yours for your daughter's hand."

Tog rubbed his hands over his belly and pretended to think. Og watched Tog's eyes. He could not hide his longing for the beautiful, large horns. Og had polished them until they almost glowed in the firelight. Tog would never be offered anything so fine for Gem's hand by the other cave dwellers.

"Give me the horns," Tog demanded.

"Not unless I can have Gem."

Tog waved to his daughter. "Gem, step forward."

"Yes, Father." Gem's voice shook. Og smiled when she clutched her hands behind her back.

"Og has asked for your hand," Tog informed her as if she knew nothing. "How do you feel about this man? Is he worthy?"

Og prayed to Tec Gem would be very careful how she answered, or it would all be over. Her father was a hard man to deal with in the best of times. Og held his breath, waiting…waiting. His mouth ached to grin. He knew what the wait was doing to him. He could only imagine what it was doing to Gem.

"Whatever you decide, my Father," she said finally. "Og is a good man. I can see he will be a good provider." She stopped, took a breath, and gave Og a slight smile. "I think he will do well as my mate. He might even be willing to help take care of you in your old age."

Og sucked in air. She may have gone too far. Cave dwellers did not like being reminded of how fragile life was, nor how short. Her father would surely be offended!

Tog studied the skins and horns for a long moment. Even Let began to shuffle his feet nervously.

"All right, she is yours." Tog glared up at the larger man. "Treat her well or her mother will be very angry."

"Yes. I know about mothers." Holding out his hand to Gem, Og said, "Come, girl. My fire burns low. You need to tend it, or I will freeze."

Gem took his hand, and her lower lip twitched. She was going to laugh.

Og gave her hand a gentle yank and pulled her toward his fire before she said or did anything to make Tog change his mind.

* * * *

Gem tended the fire and sat next to her new mate. She stared at the soft hairs on his bare leg for a moment before stroking a hand down his warm thigh. "Og?"

"Yes, Gem?"

"We will fuck now."

"Fuck? I don't understand the word."

She grinned. "You will find out soon. I will tell you, it means to share your man-shaft. Your cock. We will mate. Fuck."

"Oh. Yes. We will fuck."

Gem's heart raced. "Now!"

"Later, girl. I am busy."

She laughed softly, and her hand crept higher on his thigh. "No. You are not busy."

Her hand moved under his apron, and Og's cock swelled. The hood covering his hard knob retreated, leaving his cock naked and vulnerable. She ran a finger over the tip, and a drop of his man-juice wet her finger. With a lust-filled smile, she put her finger in her mouth.

Og's cock pushed aggressively against his apron. "I am busy," he said, but his voice quivered slightly, tellingly.

"So am I," she agreed.

Clasping his swollen cock, she stood, forcing him to stand, too. "We will go to our sleeping pallet now, my mate."

Inside the sleeping cave, she backed him until he fell, sprawling across the pile of bear skins.

His laugh filled the small cave. "I am busy, my mate."

"I do not think so, Og, but you will be soon."

She knelt next to him and placed her lips gently on his. He stared into her eyes. When she lifted her lips, Og asked, "What was that?"

"That was a kiss. It shows how much I care for you. Do you like it?"

"Oh, yes. Please do it again."

Gem touched her lips to his again and kissed him with even more meaning. She ran her tongue around his mouth. He stuck his tongue out and touched hers with his. It was exciting. Gem pushed her tongue into his mouth, and his met hers. They played for a few moments until Og was groaning.

Gem untied his apron and threw it into the corner. Her dress followed, and before Og could say a word, she was lying on top of his body. She squirmed, wiggling and giggling.

Og put his hands on her shoulders and lifted her so he could look into her eyes. "What are you doing, woman?"

"I have longed to rub my body against yours and feel the golden hair brush against my skin. It tickles."

"I don't know what 'tickle' means, but it feels good to have you lying on me. I like the way your teats feel against my chest."

He lifted her higher and licked her nipples until she was squirming and begging for more.

Og lifted her higher and held her over his burgeoning cock.

Gem slapped him hard on his chest. "Put me down."

Og was so shocked, he put her down next to his body. He held on to her with an arm around her waist. "What is wrong?"

"Before you become my husband for life, I need to know if you slept with Hoe."

Og gulped. "When would I have time? I have been very busy hunting and tanning hides to buy you from your father."

Gem wiggled around until she was facing Og. "The night we cleaned the large antelope skin, I saw Hoe climbed into your bed. Did you fuck her?"

Og laughed, and Gem slapped his chest, which only made him laugh louder. She pulled herself out of his arms and jumped out of their bed. "Well, did you?"

Og drew a deep breath and stopped laughing. "You didn't keep watching, did you?"

Gem shook her head. "No. I wanted to kill her, so I didn't look."

Og took her hand and tugged her back beside him. "If you had watched a moment longer, you would have seen me kick her out of bed and chase her away. I haven't seen her since."

Gem covered her eyes, but the tears of joy seeped out between her fingers. "I am sorry, Og. I shouldn't have doubted you. I do not trust Hoe."

Og pulled her face down and kissed her very gently. "Is there a word for how I feel about you? It is inside and it aches to be let free. I feel like running and laughing and holding you."

"I feel the same, Og. I don't know a word for the feelings, but we will think of one."

Og sat up. Using extra skins he made a padding for his back so he could lean against the rock wall. His cock pointed to the ceiling, and

Gem grinned. She leaned over him and licked his length, sucking on the large bulbous end.

"Enough," he grunted and put his hands around her waist and lifted her. Holding her high over his cock, he told her, "Open your legs, my Gem."

She did and whimpered. "Be careful. You are large and might hurt me."

"I will be very careful. I will not hurt you." His eyes told Gem he was going to treat her gently now and forever. She trusted him with her life.

He lowered her slowly over his large penis, raising her and lowering her several times before warning her, "I will fuck you now." Og groaned as her cunt rubbed oh-so-softly on the wet knob of his cock. Legs spread, opening her body for him, she took charge by placing her knees on the bed and lowering her body until his knob was touching the lips of her cunt, then she raised herself. "This is nice. Yes?"

"Oh, Tec, yes."

He lowered her until his knob was inside her.

"Touch my titties," she begged. He clasped his large hands over her breasts and suckled her nipples to hard peaks.

She sank down slowly, slowly until he was all the way inside her She tightened her internal muscles until she had his shaft captured. Her mate groaned. Gem felt joy spread through her like the rays of Tec or the warmth of a heated pool.

He suckled hard at her teats. First one and then the other. When he wasn't suckling on a nipple, he was pinching the other lightly. Gem moaned and raised her hips until his cock was barely inside her and then slowly sank down on him, each time taking him deeper. Soon, they were moving in a rhythm as old as time.

* * * *

Tec marched across the sky four times before they left their cave for a day of hunting. He could barely walk, and she was grinning like the cave fool.

Every night Gem asked Og if they could fuck, and every night Og would say, "I'm busy."

Gem would laugh against his mouth and wiggle her body against his and soon he would be begging her to wrap her hands and lips around his cock. "I know, my Og. You will always be busy and it all because of me." She would then nuzzle his male nipples until he squirmed and moaned.

Then she would push him down on their sleeping pallet, climb up to hover over his cock, and lower her body until they were joined. "Now we will fuck."

"I think I'm busy."

"Yes," she said, every time. "You're busy with me."

THE END

SIREN PUBLISHING *Allure*

LET

CHERIE DENIS

Caveman Love

LET

Caveman Love 2

CHERIE DENIS
Copyright © 2011

Let hid behind several boulders and watched with longing as Cia and Gem, her sister-friend, took their morning dip in the steam pool.

Tec, the god of light and warmth, had barely poked his nose over the cliffs, and the air was still chilled enough to raise bumps on Let's usually smooth brown arms.

Cia leaned forward and kissed the tip of Gem's heavy, round tit. Let's cock plumped and stirred against his thigh. He ached to join the young women, but he had not been invited. He was certainly old enough—his mother told him she was sure he was now eighteen summers. Old enough to experience his first mating and to take a mate for life.

He had waited and waited for the day when he would not be too young. His massive cock also proved he was old enough. Long, slender, brown fingers slid down his firm waist to grasp his man-shaft and balls. Hefting the swollen, aching appendage, he began to stroke himself.

The young women continued to play in the pool as Let watched and stroked. Soon, his man-juices spurted against the rocks, leaving a heavy, white streak down the face of the boulder.

Let sighed. He dared not groan. They would hear him and might report him to the elders. Let didn't want to speculate what punishment might befall him if the women caught him spying on them. Surely they would not scream, except possibly in playfulness.

It was now acceptable to sit at his mother's fire pit and watch as the cave-women walked about naked or nearly naked. The fact that women wandered around naked never seemed to bother his mother, who also never wore much covering, especially in the warm months. It was when his cock reacted by arching and spewing man-juice that his mother became angry and threatened to toss him out on his own.

She thought he should learn to control his shaft. If other men could, then he could also.

Well, he couldn't. That's all there was to it. He could not control how he felt about Cia and the other young women of the cave. He wanted them all, and given half a chance, he would mate with them all.

Let's attention was pulled back to the women in the pool. Cia was stroking Gem's teat, making Gem moan. The moan rose and fell like the wind when Cia's hand dropped below the water level and disappeared from sight.

Let knew what she was doing and wished he could do it to Cia.

Ah, Cia, his soon-to-be mate. She had promised herself to him when he was only a small child. She had said they would mate as soon as he reached his eighteenth summer. How many more passings of the moon would he have to wait? The moon of tiny yellow flowers had bloomed and died, a reminder that the cold months were past. The moon of the green leaves had come and gone. Now, the trees were filled out and shaded the clan as the god of light, Tec, grew stronger and stronger. The moon of sweet berries was here now.

His mother said it was his birth month. Finally, he was old enough to take a mate. Cia.

Let had to believe his mother about his birth month because his mother and father had found him sleeping under a tree many, many moons ago. His new mother guessed that when they found him he was almost forty-eight moons old. It had taken her a long time and a great deal of marking on the ground to decide his birth moon. Since he could no longer remember when they had found him, his mother was always right.

Now, Let unfurled three fingers as he counted. Only three more passings of Tec and it would be official, he would be eighteen. The elders would then let him mate with Cia. He couldn't wait. They would mate for as long as Cia would have him or until death took one of them.

The problem was that when Cia had been just a small child, the clan shaman had told her mother and father that one day she would have her own clan.

Let worried so much about whether the elders would let them mate that Cia had approached the elders about mating with Let not long ago, and they saw no problem with the mating of Cia and Let. The elders felt Let was a strong man and would be a perfect mate for Cia.

Cia had told Let that one day she would have her own clan, and she wondered if he would be bothered by her being a leader. Let hadn't taken long to decide he cared for Cia as more than just a friend, and he promised to be her help-mate.

One day, they would have their own clan, but in the meantime, they had to wait until he was old enough to join with Cia. He was very happy he would soon have her and wouldn't have to spill his seed on the ground.

Let ran a hand over his flat, firm belly. Three passings of Tec were manageable. It was a bearable amount of time. After all, he'd been waiting many summers for this day to arrive. He could wait a few more days. His cock probably didn't agree, but he would simply have to relieve himself more often. It would help the time to pass.

The only other things he had to pass the time were hunting with his friend Og and drawing on the walls of the cave.

From the pool came the sounds of Cia and Gem enjoying themselves. Gem murmured and moaned. The water rippled and rolled as the two writhed against each other's slippery bodies. They reminded him of two playful otters he'd seen in the nearby river rubbing against each other.

Let spewed his man-juice on the ground twice more before the women were finished with their play. Eventually, Gem rubbed her nose against Cia's and climbed out of the pool to dry her body with a large rabbit skin. Cia rose from the water, and Let sighed. She was so beautiful with the golden drops of water running off her body.

Drops rolled down her tits and shimmered on the tips.

His cock was getting sore from the chafing of his work-hardened hands, and yet he couldn't stop. It was Cia. He needed her. He needed her body, her heat against him under a bearskin rug at night by his fire. He felt something deep inside, a feeling he couldn't explain or name. Maybe Cia would have a name for what he was feeling.

Let was almost relieved to watch Cia and Gem leave the pool and walk back toward the cave. He had blown his seed so many times he was drained dry, leaving the ground around his feet slick with man-juice and his cock aching.

He wasn't sure he could go on like this much longer. He was wasting a lot of baby-making juice. Juices he should be sharing with Cia.

Beautiful Cia.

Her long, dark hair streamed down her back, nearly touching her muscular thighs. Her hair always reminded Let of the waterfall rolling over the cliffs after a summer rain, and the color was much like his morning drink, a brew his mother made of dark beans and water. No, the color was more like the fur of the finest antelope as it ran across the plain under the bright light of the setting of Tec.

No one knew Let had touched Cia's hair many times, and no one but Cia knew how much he hungered for her. The only thing the cave-dwellers knew about them was that one day, they would mate, and soon after, Cia would become leader of her own clan.

Let

No one stopped them from working together on Let's drawings. Let would use charcoal to draw, and Cia colored in the drawings with something she called paint. She made the paints from different berries and insects.

They had chosen the smallest cave at the end of the large main cave for their workroom. When they were there, no one bothered them, and he could touch Cia's hair and stroke her soft skin as often as she would let him. Cia told him soon he would be able to take off his work apron and stand naked so she could draw him.

"No one will know," she had told him. He wanted her to draw his body now, but Cia said they would be breaking sacred rules and both could be in deep trouble if they were found and she might lose her chance to have her own clan

Only a few more passings of Tec and Cia would be able to have him drop his apron, and she would draw him with his cock in his hand. The drawing would be very specific, showing drops of his man-juice hitting the ground.

Yes. He would shoot his man-juice on the ground then, too. It was impossible to control himself when he was near Cia. She was more beautiful than Tec, more beautiful than the little flowers blooming in the yellow flower moon.

Her hair, so soft and smooth, smelled of flowers and herbs from the special washing mixture Gem made for her, and her skin smelled of summer and rain. Let could have spent a thousand passings of the moon smelling her skin. He would never tire of her scent or her feel under his long, dark fingers.

He shouldn't think of touching her skin because even thinking of her made his cock hard. He was going to shoot more man-juice into the ground. What a waste.

Her skin was a man-tempting shade similar to the sands on the edge of the river cutting through the valley of the cave-dwellers. Her skin shimmered like the mica shards littering the sands. And the most wondrous thing about her skin was it was nearly fur free—unlike many of the elder women of the caves. Cia and the younger women only had fur guarding their woman parts. He began to wonder if Cia would let him stroke her fur today. No. She was afraid of the elders finding them.

Cia was far more beautiful than any other woman in the caves, except, perhaps, for Gem, and Gem was mated to Let's brother-friend, Og. Gem was pretty, but Let would rather think about Cia. Cia with eyes as dark and deep as the eyes of a wounded doe. Cia of the sweet skin and smooth teats.

He was not worried about Cia becoming clan leader. She was a strong, beautiful woman. She had been born to be a leader.

She was so special. Let found it hard to believe she cared so much for him.

* * * *

Cia was aware Let was watching. She was always aware of him.

No matter what he was doing or where he was going, she knew.

He was so much a part of her already that there was no guessing. She simply knew.

She also was well aware he was relieving his cock, wasting his man-juices behind the boulders. Poor Let. He was so ready to be mated, but until the elders declared Let of age, their mating was forbidden.

Cia grabbed Gem's hand. "He is watching," she whispered with a giggle.

"How do you know?"

"I can feel his eyes on me. They are as hot as my mother's fire. Don't you feel them?"

Gem laughed, throwing her long, cloud-colored hair behind her. "No, but then I'm not aching for Let. I ache for Og. It's been a long time since he put his cock in me."

Cia squeezed her friend's hand. "How long?"

"Since we woke this morning," Gem admitted with a shy smile.

"Oh, is that all? I thought it had been many passings of Tec the way you were acting."

Gem's cheeks turned as pink as her nipples. "No. It seems much longer to me."

"So tell me," Cia said as they neared the cave entrance, "how does his cock feel inside you?"

Gem's face turned a shade brighter. "I do not have words yet to tell you."

"We will think of words for it. Yes?"

"Yes."

They stood in the warming light of Tec. "I can't wait much longer for Let," Cia whispered. "Have you noticed his cock in the mornings when he walks to the scat cave?"

Gem nodded. "He is almost as big as Og."

Cia pushed her friend. "Oh, no, my sister, you are wrong. He is bigger than Og."

"No!" Gem pushed back.

"Yes." Cia gave Gem a funny smile. "Shall we make them stand together and see who is bigger?"

"I think, my sister, we should wait until you are mated. We do not want to cause the elders to become angry for any reason. Not only would you lose Let, you might ruin your chances to become leader of your own clan. Og and I can't wait for you to become leader so we may join your clan. Do not take a chance. You were meant to be Let's mate, and it's only a matter of a few more passings of Tec. You can wait as I waited for Og."

Cia's forehead wrinkled in thought. "You are right. I must be mated to Let. He is mine. I have waited since childhood for him." She turned and looked over Gem's shoulder. "Look, Gem. There goes Let now. See how long and fine his legs are and how dark, smooth, and broad his back. He is so beautiful."

Gem turned and watched Let stride across the valley floor. He was…what word would express Let's beauty? "He is very large for his age. I think a good word would be 'massive,'" she managed to express.

"Massive?" Cia seemed puzzled.

"Large. Like the Mastodon…massive."

"Oh. Yes. He is massive. All over."

"Mmmm."

The women watched until Let was a small, dark dot in the distance. Then, arms around each other's waists, they strolled into the cave.

Cia stopped at her mother's fire pit, and Gem continued on to Og's sleeping cave. Cia's mother, Fa, was resting. Her belly bulged with the child she was soon to deliver. "Are you well, Mother?"

Fa smiled, nodded and signed, "It will be soon. Is your father near?"

Cia peered about the main cave. "No, Mother, he is not inside. I think he is hunting."

"Send someone for him. I told him not to go far today. The child is near. My belly aches and rolls. It will be tonight." Her hands rubbed at her swollen belly in a soothing rhythm.

"I will get Gem's mother, Ret. She will help you."

"Yes, go, girl."

So by the setting of Tec, she would have a new sister or brother. Cia had been the only child of Fa and Dec. Her mother had given birth five finger-counts, and none had lived past a few minutes. This time, her mother had been very careful, eating only the freshest meats and vegetables. She'd drunk only boiled water, sipped fruit teas, and rested. She had every hope this child would live.

Cia didn't really care one way or another. She worried about her mother's health, but babies were loud and often in the way. It was much more fun to think about Let and his fine, long, dark cock.

Let

She stopped at Ret's fire and told her of the impending birth. Ret banked her fire, gathered her few birthing instruments and a large, carved pot to boil water in, and made her way to Fa's fire. She laid her tools carefully on a clean, tanned rabbit fur and took the pot outside to fill it with clear water. Back inside, she pushed the pot close to the fire. It would be boiling by the time she needed water for the birth.

Cia waited until her mother was busy at Fa's fire, then she gathered her own tools. Today, she would work on the drawings she had started in the small side cave she and Let would occupy when she mated with him. It would soon be their home and their fire. She was so excited. She could barely wait for the day they would be mated.

She'd been thinking about their mating a lot lately and knew she was not going to wait until the elders said it was time. She wanted Let, and he wanted her. She was going to mate with him today. He was eighteen summers old now, and she had waited long enough.

Let would come to her after he'd hunted for a time. He always did. He couldn't stay away from her, and she did not discourage him. She wanted and needed him near. When Let was with her, she felt safe. She also felt things she could not describe because she still didn't have the words to do so.

Words were so special to her. She and Gem had been working on making up words for things since they were girls. After each new discovery, they taught the words to the other young cave-dwellers. The elders used hand signals much of the time and refused to learn to speak. However, Gem's mother could and would speak once in a while if the mood struck her, which wasn't often because it made her mate angry.

Cia checked to be sure she had her special drawing tools and her paints, and with a burning stick in hand, she headed to the cave she and Let would someday make their home.

* * * *

Let's long, strong legs took him across the plain quickly. He'd forgotten his spear, but he wasn't worried. Within minutes of leaving the safety of the home cave, Let came upon a straight branch as tall as he. Lifting it, he hefted it a few times. It was well balanced and would make a perfect hunting tool. Next, he scoured the ground for a piece of obsidian. If he couldn't find a piece, he would have to return to the cave, and he would look foolish to the elders.

He was about to give up when he found a piece. It wasn't shaped quite right, but a little effort on his part and it would be perfect.

A piece of volcanic rock in his large hand did a fine job of shaping the tip for his new spear. From the pouch he carried around his waist, Let pulled a long piece of sinew and quickly attached the now-sharpened piece of shining, black rock to the shaft.

Balancing the shaft on his shoulder, Let took off at a slow lope across the plain.

Several days ago, Let had seen a large antelope. Such a giant animal would make the perfect gift for Cia. It would furnish her family with many meals, and it would impress her father. It was not as large as the one Og had killed to win Gem as a mate, but the fleet animal Let had seen was still quite beautiful and fat.

Let's cock brushed against his thigh as he ran, reminding him of his hunger for Cia—a hunger he could not seem to be rid of, no matter how hard he tried.

He loped along at a steady pace, his eyes ever alert for the animal, but his heart and body called out for Cia.

He knew where she was at this very moment, and he couldn't wait to be with her. He hoped by the time he found the animal, she would still be working and waiting for him.

Let sighed and prayed to Tec for guidance and strength. Tec did not fail him. Soon, he came upon the antelope. As he crept closer to his prey, Let realized it was even larger than he had remembered.

One well-placed thrust of his spear and the animal dropped dead where it stood. Quickly, Let lifted the animal, draped it over his shoulders like a cloak, and began to make his way back to the cave. He wanted to get the animal back as soon as possible so the women could drain it. Tonight, there would be blood soup for the evening meal—a delicacy they all craved but seldom could enjoy.

Later, he would skin and gut the carcass. Then he would get it ready for the women to cure. Recently, some of the cave women had found a salt pool, and by pure chance, they had soaked some meat in the brine and dried it. The meat had not spoiled as it often did. The brine pool had been a wondrous find for them all. To be able to save more meat would mean fewer of the dwellers would die over the white months.

Let's mother was huddled over her fire brewing herb tea when he stopped and told her about the animal waiting outside the cave. Let was still telling her his hunting story when his mother jumped up, gathered up her bowls and obsidian knives, and rushed out to bleed the animal. Let stared after her. He hadn't finished his hunting story.

Cia would listen. She loved his stories.

Let's mother would be gone for some time. Now, he could go to Cia. It was early. She would still be there, waiting for him and working on her drawings.

Everyone in the cave was either busy at a fire or out hunting. The central cave was silent because the smaller children were sleeping. Two older women had followed his mother outside to help bleed the antelope. No one was paying attention to him, which meant Let was free to go to Cia.

* * * *

Cia was putting the finishing touches on a new drawing of Let when he spoke behind her.

"I have come, girl."

She jumped. She had been thinking of him, and suddenly he was with her. She turned and greeted him with a smile. He was closer than she'd thought. He was so close she could smell his man-smell and feel his heat. Cia's face grew hot. She wanted him so much. She could not wait for their official mating.

Let stepped closer and rubbed his nose on Cia's. She sucked in a deep breath and without thinking touched her lips to his. Lip touching was not accepted practice for the un-mated.

Why shouldn't they touch lips? It was lovely and made her cunt wet and her belly feel hollow.

The touch of his lips on hers always thrilled her and made her cunt swell with hunger. He was the first man she had touched lips with. The other men she had only fucked to learn how to be a good mate.

The first time she had touched her lips to his, Let had stepped back, nearly falling. His beautiful, dark face had turned pale. It had startled them both, but the second time had been better, and the third had set off a fire inside both of them. Cia had barely been able to keep from mating with him.

Let had been more alert than Cia. He had eventually put his hands on her shoulders and pushed her gently away. His cock had stood out from his belly like a tree trunk from the earth.

"I…I…I…"

"Yes?"

"What did we do, Cia?" Let had asked.

"Gem calls it kissing. Do you like it?"

He had nodded.

"Good. I think we should do it again."

Let had grinned and opened his arms. Cia had leaned close to him and touched her lips to his. This time, the lip touching had lasted a lot longer and made Cia feel funny in her cunt.

She had stepped even closer to Let and trapped his cock between them. His hot cock had burned against her belly, branding her for life.

Now, every time they were alone, Cia kissed Let, and Let kissed back. He was a quick learner, which pleased Cia greatly. He was going to make a fine mate and partner of a clan leader.

Cia wanted to giggle. Kissing was exciting not only for her. Let was enjoying it, too, because as always, his cock was becoming hard, hot, and large against her. His broad, dark hands rose and covered her tits. Gem had called her tits "breasts" today in the pool. Cia liked the new word.

"Yes," she moaned against Let's mouth. "Touch my breasts."

Let opened his eyes and moved his head a fraction of an inch. "A new word? 'Breasts'?"

Cia put her hands over his and pressed. "Yes, these are breasts. Do you like my breasts?"

Let groaned and gave her breasts a gentle squeeze. "Oh, yes. I like your breasts." He pinched her nipples, which immediately responded by tightening into firm beads. "What are these?"

"You like feeling them, don't you, Let?"

"Yes. What are they?" He swept a rough finger over the tip of her breasts.

"Ahhhh." Cia writhed under his fingers. "Nipples. They are nipples."

"Oh. I will taste," Let demanded, leaning close. He didn't wait for her agreement. His long tongue flicked out and touched the tip of one nipple, and Cia's legs trembled. Her cunt began to weep, the honey running down the inside of her thigh.

No man affected her like Let could. She had relieved many men of their man-juice when they'd demanded her attention, but none of them were as wonderful as Let.

It was accepted by the cave-dwellers that if a man's cock needed relief and his mate was not available, either because she was bleeding or had just given birth, he could demand attention from any woman in the cave.

Cia was acknowledged as an excellent relief-giver.

Let's cock brushed against her belly, and Cia reached down to touch him. His skin was so hot, slick, and smooth. She couldn't wait to taste his man-juice and to feel his cock slide into her cunt.

Let continued to be mesmerized by her breasts and nipples. This was the first time she had let him touch her, and he didn't have enough words to tell her how he was feeling.

Her fingers pushed back the hood covering his cock, and drops of man-juice wet her hand. She smoothed the man-juice over the tip of his cock, and Let's hips bucked.

"Yes," Let groaned against her mouth. "Yes, Cia. Touch me more."

"Like this?" Cia stroked his long cock slowly. Her single hand was not large enough to fit around his cock, but her other hand was busy stroking his firm balls.

"Ahhh." Let groaned and began to sink to the floor of the cave. Since his long fingers still clasped her breasts, Cia followed him down, anxious to continue. The game they were playing was dangerous and could get them both punished. No one mated until the elders gave their approval and they had not received official approval. The cave floor was colder than the white moisture that covered the plains in the winter moons, and Cia shivered when her knees hit the ground. Let groaned, and Cia whispered, "Keep silent, or we will be found, Let."

She couldn't afford to be caught sucking Let's man-shaft. If she broke the rules, the elders might forbid her to mate with Let or any other man. She couldn't bear to lose Let. He was the mate of her soul.

He was no longer a boy. Let was a man, full grown and larger than any of the cave dwellers in their cave. Larger than any caveman in the other caves of the valley. Women from other caves had told her there was no man as large, as strong, or as beautiful as Let.

Let was special.

No one was positive how many summers Let had. His mother had found him crying under a tree, and she had counted many lines in the sand to try to figure out his age. Cia had a feeling he was a lot older than his mother thought. He had a man's body and a man's mind.

Cia prayed to Tec that she was not breaking any cave rules, because she was anxious to have her own clan. Rules, or no rules, she couldn't stop her feelings for Let. Her mouth watered at the thought of tasting his man-juice. With the hood of his shaft pushed back and out of the way, the head of his cock shone dark and wet. She smoothed her forefinger over the weeping eye of his cock. Let moaned.

She placed her mouth over his to stifle his groan, and again she was shocked at the feelings traveling through her body at the touch of his full, dark lips. "Oh, Let. I must fuck you."

Let's long fingers pulled at her nipples, tugging hard. It hurt, but it was a delicious pain. She wished he would do it harder. Before she could ask him, Let whispered, "Yes, Cia. Fuck me like you fuck Tog and Sen and all the other men. I have watched you from afar, and I watch the other men's faces when you take their cocks inside. You make them all happy. I want to be happy."

She squeezed his cock lightly. "You will be happier than any of those men, Let. You will see. You are very special to me. Not like those men. I will make you very, very happy. I will fuck you and suck on your cock and taste you until you are out of man-juice."

Let's large, white teeth sparkled in the firelight. "Yes. We will do it now?"

Cia frowned. No. There was too great a chance they would get caught and her father would forbid her to take Let as her mate. Still, no one had found them yet. What would it matter if she had just one taste of his cock?

She pressed his muscular body down onto the rough cave floor, and Let protested weakly but lay back as she'd directed.

"Be quiet," she demanded. "I will taste your cock, and then you must go. We cannot get caught."

Let arched his back, telling her wordlessly of his willingness. His cock jutted high and straight from his body. Cia tangled her fingers in the kinky fur guarding his cock and gave a light tug.

Everything about Let was so different from all the other men in the cave. Her friend Gem's mate, Og, was also different from all the other men. Og was light-skinned, and his fur was also light and shining. He was like the light Tec gave off each day, bright and glorious. Og was a beautiful man and a perfect mate for her friend and sister Gem.

Let was as dark as the bark on a tree, and his fur was even darker and very sparse. His face was smooth and soft. His mouth was dark and firm—the same as his beautiful cock. The fur guarding Let's cock was tightly curled and crisp as the grass after the white cold fell from the sky. But nothing about Let was cold. He was hot. Hot to the touch and hot to be near. His massive body gave off a heat all its own—a heat that rivaled the warmth of her home fire.

The other men of the cave were of many differing colors of the earth, and most of the older men were heavily furred. The younger men were lightly covered with all types of fur. Some were crisp, some silky, and some had both types of fur.

The men also were different when it came to their cocks. Some were as short and fat as the men who owned the cocks. Some were long and thin, some heavy and full. All were hooded to prevent injury when they ran or hunted.

She would push back the hood and taste them. Some tasted nasty—a word she and Gem had invented long ago—and some tasted like herbs. Some she didn't even want to think about. Few tasted good enough to enjoy.

Cia only did what was demanded of her and never found it pleasant to talk about.

Cia bent over Let, and while he played with her nipples, she ran a finger over the eye of his cock. His juice slicked over the head of his cock, and Let groaned. "Quiet, Let," she whispered. "Be very quiet. I will taste now…"

Her tongue touched the slit of his shaft, and silently Let arched off the floor. She ran her tongue around the bulging head of his cock, and Let opened his mouth. She put two fingers over his mouth as a warning. He sank back silently.

Let wasn't playing with her nipples, and Cia wanted that to continue. She let loose of his shaft and balls and put his hands back on her breasts. "Touch me," she ordered. When he did, she went back to what she'd been doing—playing with his cock.

She closed both hands around his throbbing shaft and bent to her task. Let would not lie quietly. He continued to writhe and wiggle, much like the snakes living in the forest. Cia licked the cap of his cock. Let groaned.

He tasted wonderful, like the fresh grasses growing along the river. Sweet, slick, and a bit tart.

Let's cock grew in length and breadth. How could that be? He was already larger than any man she'd ever seen, yet he continued to grow larger and firmer. His balls also continued to grow larger and firmer as he neared explosion.

Cia ran her hands up and down his slick shaft, silently urging him to finish.

His cock seemed to be gathering strength, shuddering and trembling with each stroke of her hands. More of his man-juice oozed out of his slit, wetting Cia's fingers and making her movements easier.

Up. Down. Up. Down.

"Yes," Let groaned, and his hips came off the floor.

Cia opened her mouth to catch his man-juice and was rewarded when he exploded.

Man-juice shot high into the air in great globs and fell back to earth with tiny splats. It sounded like water falling from the sky on a dark day. Cia caught some of the drops in her mouth, and when his man-juice slowed, she closed her mouth over his trembling cock and caught as much as she could. Soon, his juice ran out of the corners of her mouth and landed in a shallow pool on Let's smooth, dark belly.

"Cia? Where are you, girl?"

Gem. If Gem caught her with Let's cock in her mouth, Cia knew they would not be in trouble. But if one of the elders found them, she, not Let, would be punished.

Thank the god, Tec, it was Gem.

Cia lifted her head and wiped her mouth with the back of her hand. Swallowing quickly, she stood and rushed to the doorway of the small sleeping cave, leaving Let still shooting his juices toward the rounded ceiling of the cave.

Cia shifted her leather work apron to cover her cunt and ran her hands over her aching, swollen breasts. Gem would know what she'd been doing. There was nothing she could do to hide her upper body. Perhaps she should have Gem's mother make her some of the woven coverings she'd made to hide Gem's breasts.

"Yes?" Cia stopped Gem before she could walk in on Let. She took Gem's arm and led her away from the cave opening. She didn't want Gem to see Let. Cia turned casually and looked back into the cave and was disappointed to realize the firelight reflected Let's shadow on the cave wall.

Let was still shooting man-juice skyward.

Cia pulled her friend farther away from the small sleeping cave. "Yes, my sister? What is wrong?"

Gem grinned. "I know what you're doing, girl."

"Yes? And?"

Gem's grin grew, and she stroked a warm hand over Cia's swollen breasts. "And Og and I would join you if we had time, but we do not."

Cia was puzzled. "You would join us?"

Gem nodded. "Oh, yes. I'm sure we would have fun, but you must go now."

"Go? Now? Why?"

Gem laughed. "There's no time for fucking, girl. Your mother is giving birth while we stand here talking."

"Oh. I will tell Let. Wait for me."

"I would see Let, yes?"

"No!" Cia growled. "No. You will not see Let. He is mine, and I will not share him."

"Why not? Is he not good?"

"I haven't taken him for a mate yet. I do not know if he is good, and I will not let you find out. Do you want to share Og?"

Gem grinned. "No, not yet. But one time, we will share a cave and see who has the best mate."

Cia shrugged her shoulders. "Maybe one day, but not today. Where is Og?" Cia asked before she returned to her lover.

Gem laughed. "He is busy."

"He is always busy." Cia also laughed.

She returned to tell Let she had to go to her mother and found him resting on his side, cock in hand. He watched her, his eyes full of fear. "We will do it again?" he asked with a bright, shining smile.

Cia's knees weakened, and her womanhood wept for Let's touch. Let was so beautiful with the firelight reflecting off his dark skin. She bent and touched her lips to his. "Yes. We will do it again. Soon, very soon."

Let rose to his knees and put his long arms around her. "Good. I am ready now." His long cock stood straight out from his body, glistening and hot to the touch. He pressed his body against Cia's belly and rubbed her with his wet cock.

"We cannot, Let. My mother is giving birth, and I must go to her now."

Let's smile fell, and his dark eyes filled with sorrow.

"Come to me tomorrow, Let, and we will draw pictures of your cock and play."

His smile brightened. "I will return."

"Now, cover yourself," Cia urged anxiously. "Gem is waiting outside to go with me to my mother's sleeping cave."

But before Let could stand to put on his leather work apron, Cia leaned forward and put her lips on the tip of his cock.

"Nice," she said softly.

Let laughed. "Your touch feels good."

"I like to lick you. We will do it again. Tomorrow."

Then she touched her lips to his and waited for him to cover his cock with his apron.

They left the sleeping cave together.

"So, my sister," Gem said with a sly peek at Let. "I see you have been busy."

Cia shrugged her shoulders. Taking Let's large hand in hers, she led them across the main cave to her mother's sleeping cave.

Gem tried several times to make Let talk about what they had been doing in the sleeping cave he and Cia would soon be sharing as mates, but Let was the strong, silent type. He merely nodded and smiled.

Cia loved Let's smile, so sweet and full of innocence. Let would tell no one. He wanted her for his mate, and he knew if he said too much too soon, they might not be able to mate.

* * * *

Cia's mother was close to delivery. She groaned and thrashed her head against the bearskin under her body. Because she was the eldest and only daughter, it was to be Cia's privilege to cut the baby's cord when it made its way into the light of Tec.

Cia helped Fa to rise and eased her swollen body onto the birthing chair Cia's father, Dec, had carved in expectation of this special birth. This was the sixth time Cia would cut the cord of a new child, but unlike the other births, this time, the child would live and grow. Fa had delivered too early each of the other times, but this time, Fa had carried the child a full nine moons.

This child would grow and flourish. Praise Tec.

All the dwellers anxiously awaited the birth of this special child. All knew the story of Fa's lost children, and all prayed to Tec for the safe delivery of this child.

Gem's mother was there to ease the delivery, and Dec paced outside the opening of the main cave. Cia knew her father was frightened for Fa's life and the life of the child. He could not bear to hear his mate cry in pain as the child entered its new home.

Cia had watched her father's face as each passing of the moon brought Fa closer to giving birth. His homely face had become more wrinkled with fear and age. He had signaled more than once to tell Cia he and Fa were too old to be having another child. Cia would have to help with the child. It would be her responsibility. He did not want his mate burdened or overworked. All he wanted Fa to do was rest and feed the child. The rest of its care would be Cia's. Cia was strong and did not mind. She needed to learn how to take care of a child anyway if she and Let were going to mate.

The older women sent Gem and Cia out of the birthing cave. The young women leaned against the cave wall, waiting silently for someone to tell them what they were to do. Giving birth was more dangerous than running from a wild boar, more life-threatening than the saber-toothed tiger. Neither young woman could think of anything to say. Both were too frightened to speak of their fears.

What if Fa died? Who would feed the child?

What if the child died? Would it kill Fa this time?

The last time, Cia and Gem had searched the forest floor for herbs to ease Fa's suffering. Could they find more of the mood-lifting herb if she needed it this time? They had saved some from the last time, but it would not last long enough for the next growing season.

Fa's legs were spread wide over the opening in the birthing stool, her feet flat on the cave floor. Her face, dark as the sky before a storm, was scrunched up in pain. Fa held her breath and grunted. Again and again she pushed. She groaned and moaned, yet nothing happened. Ret urged her with hand signals to push harder.

Ret signaled she could see the fur on the top of the baby's head as it pressed its way out of Fa's woman-opening.

Fa gave a hard push followed by a loud grunt, and the child's head popped out.

The child's eyes were closed. Its little nose was flat and squashed against its small, round face.

Cia moved forward, anxious to do her part in this momentous occasion.

Ret dipped her instruments in the boiling water she had waiting by the fireside. Nothing was going to ruin this birth. This child would live.

Using her hands, Ret turned the child and eased its shoulder out of Fa. With a low moan, Fa was able to push the child out into Ret's waiting hands. Ret grasped the child by his heels and tapped him gently on the back.

A squeal filled the sleeping cave, and a joyous shout could be heard as Gem ran from the sleeping cave to notify the clan.

Dec had a new son.

Cia waited while Ret readied the cord for cutting, and then with the thin edge of a piece of mica, she cut the child loose from their mother.

"He is beautiful, my mother," Cia signaled to Fa. "What is his name?"

Fa, tired and sweaty, pushed her hair off her face and sighed. She signed for Cia to ask her father for the name he had chosen. Cia nodded. His naming would be her father's decision.

Old rules were not to be broken.

Using the water she had boiled and let cool, Ret cleaned the child. As soon as she delivered the afterbirth, she cleaned Fa and laid the child at her breast. The child was strong and fat. He immediately latched onto his mother's swollen teat and began to suckle for all he was worth.

"It is good," Ret signed to Fa. "He is strong and feeding. He will grow to be the biggest man in the clan."

Without disturbing her child, Fa checked him over from head to toe and was smiling when she looked up at Cia. "Tell Dec all is well," she signed. "Have him come now. He needs to bury the afterbirth and say many prayers of thanksgiving to Tec."

Cia rushed to find her father, who was pacing the dirt floor in front of the sleeping cave. "It is a son, and he is well, my father," Cia signed. "Ret tells us he will grow to be the largest man in the clan."

Dec, who seldom showed any emotion, laughed and rubbed at his eyes. "It is good," he signed. "I will go in now?"

"Yes, my mother waits for you to see the boy and name him."

* * * *

Let sat at his mother's fireside, staring across the cave at Cia. Cia spent a good deal of each passing of Tec tending to her new baby brother. Little Sin was now one moon old, and Cia's mother relied on her daughter for a great deal of help. Poor Fa was still recovering from Sin's birth. She spent most of her time resting and rocking back and forth while she fed and held him.

The other women of the cave helped Cia as much as they could, but they, too, had families to tend to, fires to stoke, and men to keep happy.

Let stroked his cock and wished Cia had some time for him. His cock ached, and he was still waiting for the promise she had made the day Sin was born.

Cia had said they would enjoy the touch of each other's bodies again, and they had not. His cock was getting tired of waiting. He wanted Cia. He hungered for her. He wanted to feel the touch of her lips on the tip of his cock. She had done it once, and he wanted it to happen again.

Let stood, and his cock thrust its way toward the high roof of the cave.

Enough. He would no longer wait.

He put on his work apron, but it did little to cover his massive cock.

"Let?"

"Yes, my mother?"

"Where are you going?"

"To Cia," he growled.

"You should wait for her signal," his mother groused. She was busy stirring a pot of something for his evening meal. It smelled of spices and sage and was probably the large bird he had captured and killed with a rock this very day.

"I can wait no longer, my mother. I am now eighteen summers, and I am tired of waiting for her to call me to her bed." Let smoothed his hand down the front of his work apron.

His cock jumped and pulsed. "I am very tired of waiting."

"Sit, my son. Eat your meal. Be patient. She will call you to her bed soon. I have spoken to Fa and Dec, and they are as anxious as you."

"Do you see my cock, Mother?"

She nodded without lifting her eyes from the simmering pot.

"Well, it, too, is tired of waiting. I go." He took a step toward Cia's home fire, and his mother put out a hand.

"You should wait…"

"No." His voice echoed through the main cave. Many heads looked up to stare at his mother's home fire.

He strode across the cave, his steps long and firm. Behind him, his mother sighed and continued to stir the pot with the wooden spoon he had carved for her many moons ago. Let knew she was upset with him, but he was tired of waiting. He wanted Cia. Now.

"Cia," he spoke softly, but the baby, Sin, jumped and snuffled against Cia's breast.

Cia directed Sin's tiny lips to her nipple and gave a soft smile when he latched on. "Mmm?"

Let squatted across the fire from Cia so he could watch the baby's mouth suckle at her tit. Tec. She was more beautiful than the flowers of summer. The baby sucked hard, and Cia grimaced.

"Does it hurt?" Let asked in a gentle whisper.

"A little. There is no milk. He is just happy sucking, and my mother is so tired. I sent her to lie down."

"Does it hurt when my mouth is on your tit?" His voice quivered, and Let swallowed loudly.

Cia looked directly into his eyes, an act forbidden unless a couple were mated. "No."

Let's cock rose like a tree in the forest, pushing against his work apron until he was fully exposed. "I want you, Cia. I want to be the one tasting and suckling your tits."

She nodded and looked down at her little brother. "I know," she whispered.

"How long must I wait?"

She sighed, touching her lips to Sin's dark head. "Not long, Let. Only a few more passings of Tec. Soon, Sin will be old enough for my mother to stop worrying that he will go to live with Tec like all her other babies."

"He is strong," Let said, as much to assure himself as to ease Cia's mind.

"Yes. He is as strong as a little tiger cub," she said fondly, running a finger through the fur on the baby's head.

"I will fuck you, Cia." Let's voice was more forceful than it should have been, but he was hungry for her.

Again, she looked into his eyes with understanding. "Tonight, when the main cave is empty and the families are in their sleeping caves, I will meet you in our cave."

Let's heart flew like the bird over the river. "Tonight," he whispered, looking over his shoulder. No one was near.

She looked directly at his cock and nodded. "Tonight, Let. You are old enough now for me to take you as my mate."

Let's cock rose like the mountains surrounding the cave. Drops of man-juice formed on the tip of his cock. Cia watched as the drops fell to the cave floor.

Let smiled, and his white teeth gleamed against the dusky glow of his smooth skin. Cupping his cock and balls, he said, "It is nice?"

Cia licked her lips and nodded.

"Good. It is big. Is it big enough for you?"

Again, Cia nodded. Speech seemed to have left her for the first time since Let had met her many, many moons ago. They were both little children. He'd been sitting under a tree alone, crying. A small woman had walked up to him and signed something he did not understand, but he had stopped crying when she'd held out her hand.

Cia had been there that day, and she, too, had held out her hand to him. She was the prettiest of all the group standing around him. She had encouraged him to come with them, and from then on, there had been something special between them. The special feeling had grown as he had grown. Now, the feeling lived in his body and had taken over his life.

"Cia? Am I big enough? I have seen you fucking the older men of the cave. I worry I will not be a good enough mate." It was his greatest fear. What if he was not as big as the other men Cia had fucked?

"Stand up, Let," Cia directed.

"Others are watching," he said with a grin.

"Yes. The women will be most happy to see your large cock. Many men will be made happy tonight."

Let stood and waited.

"Open your work apron," she directed, "and set it to the side. I will look at your cock."

Let unfastened the apron and threw it on the ground. He'd barely missed the fire pit, but at the moment, he really didn't care. His cock rose impressively from the dark, curly fur guarding his balls.

Cia stared openly at his impressive, glistening cock. "You are so beautiful. Your skin is smooth and shining." Cia licked her lips. "Push your hood back and show me the tip of your cock."

Many eyes were now watching them. Let could feel the heat of those eyes, and it made him more excited. He slowly eased the hood covering the tip of his cock back to show the dark, wet tip to his mate.

"Oh, yes." She sighed. "I will mate with you tonight after all the others sleep. I don't have the words for what I feel about the beauty of your cock. Look how it glows in the firelight. Look how the tip gets wet and shines like the moon. You are more beautiful than the trees in summer, larger than the volcano, Pot, who breathes fire every moon, and hotter than the light of Tec."

Cia breathed deeply, and her nipple popped out of Sin's sleeping mouth. "You are the largest man in the cave and possibly the largest man in the valley. And you are going to be mine."

Let couldn't take his eyes off her wet nipple. Several drops of man-juice dropped into the fire and sizzled.

The cave seemed to hold its breath, waiting for what would happen next. Would Cia fuck her mate here in front of everyone? They had all been counting the passings of Tec and knew he was on the edge of his eighteenth summer.

Let cradled his large, beautiful appendage in both his long hands, keeping the hood pushed back so he could stroke the tip of his cock. His finger came away wet. "Will you lick me, as you did before?"

"Oh, yes, my mate. I will lick you and suck you. Then I will fuck you until you are limp as an old man."

Let bent and picked up his work apron.

"I will wait for you, my mate. Tonight," he whispered in parting. "Tonight."

"Yes, tonight," she agreed, touching her lips to Sin's tiny forehead. "I will fuck you until you are weak as a newborn. We will make sure you are strong enough to help lead my clan."

Let laughed, and the joyous sound echoed throughout the main cave. "We will see who is the stronger—you or me." He turned and strode away.

Cia watched his dark body leave her fireside and wanted to run after him. How she longed for him. Tonight he would become her mate for life. Cia sighed. He was going to taste more delicious than the sweetest water. The feel of his cock high inside her was a prize she had longed for since her first bleed. She had waited a very long time for this night.

"Soon, Sin. Soon, he will be mine." Cia eased her tiny brother down to nestle in the bearskin covering the cave floor near the fire. She made sure he was not too close to the heat of the fire and went to wake her mother. It was time to eat the evening meal.

* * * *

Cia helped settle Sin and her mother for the night, then she brewed a cup of herbal tea for her father. "They are asleep, Father, hopefully for the rest of the night," she signed.

He wrapped his hands around the stone cup and nodded.

Cia continued signing. "I'm going to take a swim and spend the night in my cave. Mother will be able to take care of Sin this night, and I am tired."

Dec signed that he understood. "I thank you, my daughter, for your help. Fa has been able to rest since Sin's birth, and now, she is stronger. The night is yours. Rest easy. I will take care of your mother."

"Thank you, Father." She stood staring at the rough cave floor. "Is there anything you need before I go?"

Dec smiled and his finger flew. "No. Go, my daughter."

Cia grinned. She didn't plan on getting any sleep this night.

The night was warm and close. She hurried to the hot pool and, stripping off her work apron, slipped into the warm water. Using the herb scrub Gem had taught her to make, Cia cleansed her body until her skin shone in the moonlight. Next, she washed and rinsed her hair using the honey and lemon wash Gem had made. Finally, she chewed the spicy stick Gem had told her would make her teeth clean and her mouth smell nice.

Where was Let? Was he cleaning himself for her? Many moons ago, when they were still children, Cia had taught him how to cleanse his body and mouth for his health and to please her. He was very careful to do as she said, so she wasn't worried. He would come to the mating bed looking and tasting as good as he could.

Cia's cunt was swollen and aching. It throbbed for Let's attention and his cock. She had denied many men in the cave access to her body for the last few moons so she would be pure for Let. The men of the cave had not been happy, but she was proud of her willpower. After all, she loved to fuck and had done so since she was fourteen summers old. At the time, Ret had taken her aside and showed her the herbs she would need to prevent babies. Ret had also explained the making of a sheath to cover the man's cock—another way to prevent babies. Cia was *very* knowledgeable in the ways of fucking. Now, it was time to train Let. He was smart and would learn fast.

The women of the cave told her she was too old to wait any longer for a mate. It was time to pick a mate and begin making babies. Cia agreed. She was tired of waiting for Let to be eighteen summers. Besides, since the cave-dwellers had found him as a small child, he could be even older than everyone guessed. He certainly looked like he was eighteen, and his cock was larger than any other man's in the cave.

Cia dried her body with rabbit fur and tied on a clean work apron. She took her time returning to the cave, hoping to see Let along the way.

Her home fire was banked, and her father was missing. He was probably asleep next to her mother and baby Sin. Much of the main cave was silent as many of the residents were now in their sleeping caves.

Cia heard a baby crying in one of the caves. The sound didn't last long. She was fairly sure its mother had offered up a teat to the child. Silence reigned once again. Cia bent and picked up a slender stick and put it in the banked fire. When the tip glowed and burst into flame, she lifted the stick and made her way to the cave that would soon become her new home. It wouldn't be long now before Let would join her, and she was anxious to begin the mating.

In the small sleeping cave, Cia stacked several pieces of dried grass and firewood in the fire pit. Touching her firebrand to the grass, she blew gently to get a fire going. When she had a nice flame, she sat back and watched it grow. At the right time, she added a piece of black rock to keep the fire going for hours.

The air warmed and soothed her into a dreamlike state. Where was Let? Would he come to her, or had he changed his mind? Her nipples swelled, and her woman's place began to weep as she thought about his touch. She hoped he was as hungry for her as she was for him. Would his cock be large and hard? Would it glisten with moisture? Would his protective hood be pulled back? Her cunt continued to weep pearls of fluid. The drops rolled down her thighs and pooled on the cave floor.

Heat flowed through her body. Her nipples tingled and ached for the touch of Let's tongue.

How long must she wait?

Where was Let?

* * * *

Let had learned well from his soon-to-be mate. He washed his body in the large pool reserved for men. The night was warm and caressed his body as Cia's hands would soon. His cock refused to rest and continued to point to the moon above. Let pushed back his protective hood and cleansed his cock as Cia had long ago taught him.

Drops of moisture formed on the tip, and Let smoothed them over his cock until he gleamed.

The thought of Cia's small hands on his cock and balls had him aching hard and close to eruption.

Silent and cool, the moon watched him cleanse his body.

Was Cia waiting for him? Was she resting on her bearskin bed? Were her legs open? Was her woman's place swollen and ready for him?

He should not think of Cia. He should not think about her woman's place. His eruption spewed man-juice across the pool in ball-emptying gouts of white.

Let hung his head. He shouldn't have done it, but sometimes, he couldn't stop himself. He only wondered for a moment if there was anything left for Cia. His cock revived quickly, and with relief, Let finished bathing. He walked back to the cave, fastening a clean work apron around his narrow waist as he strode toward the home caves.

The main cave was silent. A rodent chewed on a bone, its teeth making a small sound in the quiet. Let watched an ocelot cub come awake and begin stalking the rodent. A moment's scuffle and the rodent was gone. The ocelot licked its lips and returned to its sleeping mat at Sen's fire.

Let waited until the cat was settled before continuing on his way. Banked fires gave a soft glow to the stark rock walls. Pillars of stone sparkled and glistened. It was the best time of day in the cave. All but the night guards were sleeping, and the guards left Let to his journey. These men did not speak. They couldn't or wouldn't. It all depended on their age.

The older guards didn't speak because they didn't believe in words. The younger guards would speak if spoken to, but in general, the guards ignored the coming and goings of the clan. They were only to guard the cave entrance, not judge who was going where in the cave at night.

These men were not stupid. They knew what Let was up to. One of the young men gave Let the signal for fucking. He circled his forefinger and thumb and pushed the middle finger of his other hand back and forth in the circle.

Let nodded and smiled.

Yes. Tonight he was going to fuck his Cia for the first time.

It was an honor, a privilege he had earned many years ago when he and Cia had been children too young to fuck but not too young to explore each other's bodies.

More than once, they had been caught and reprimanded by the elders for their behavior. The moment the elders were busy again, Cia had been there with her hands out to touch him in the most delicious ways and tease him until Let thought he would go to join their ancestors.

A faint glow from the sleeping cave he would soon share with Cia told him she was waiting for him. He stopped in the doorway and gathered his thoughts. His cock jutted out from its resting place and lifted his work apron away from his body. Let was not shy. This was the way Cia liked to see him. She had him pose frequently with his cock in his hands. She would draw pictures of him on the walls of the sleeping-cave, and when she was done, she would lick his shaft until he spewed man-juice on her face.

"Cia?"

"Yes," she whispered in reply.

"I will come to you now?"

"I am waiting." Her voice turned Let's insides to fire.

He stepped through the opening, and the air left his body in a great whoosh.

She lay as he had imagined. She was naked on a bearskin pallet with her legs open and her woman's place weeping for his attention.

"Come closer," Cia urged.

"I will look at you first." Let smiled, and his teeth gleamed in the firelight.

Cia opened her legs wider, and Let knelt between her knees. He leaned in and took a deep breath, filling his soul with her scent. He put out his hands and gently opened her womanhood with trembling fingers. She was warm and wet inside. He started to put a finger in her cunt, but Cia moaned, and her hips lifted off the bed.

Let pulled back his hands, and his cock wilted. "Did I hurt you?"

Cia groaned. "No, Let. It is good. Do it some more, and you will see how much we both like it."

"Like this?" he asked, putting his fingers back on her cunt.

She took his thumb and showed him how to brush it across her clit. Moisture followed his fingers, smoothing the way. She shivered and let go of his hand. Let was a fast learner. She'd only had to show him once what she liked, and he knew what to do to please her.

He gently put his long, slim middle finger in her cunt and brushed across her clit. Cia bit her arm to keep from crying out. She dug her fingers in the long fur of the bear-skin.

"It is good. Yes?"

She could barely breathe. "It is better than good." He brushed across her clit again, and she trembled. Her legs dropped open wider while drops of moisture wet the bearskin under her hips. "Ohhh, yes, Let, do it again and again."

Let leaned closer, searching her secret place. "Your womanhood is as pretty as the flowers blooming in the light of Tec, and like the flowers, your petals open for my fingers. It is nice. I will taste you, Cia?"

"Yesss," she said with a sigh.

He bent forward, inhaled deeply, and his tongue flicked out to taste her honey.

"Ahhh," Cia moaned when his tongue touched her clit.

"It is good." Let growled and buried his nose in her cunt.

Cia continued to moan and writhe under his tongue and fingers. Let couldn't remember ever being this happy or this close to explosion. He felt as the volcano must feel before spewing fire. His body shook like the mountains did before such explosions. Cia, too, trembled and quivered as the ground beneath their feet often shook when the volcano was angry.

Let raised his head to stare at Cia. Licking his lips, he sighed. "I will take you now?"

Cia's eyes popped open. "No. Not yet, Let. I want to taste your cock. I want to stroke your balls. I want you to lick my breasts. I want to play all night. I don't want to waste any of your precious fluids, Let."

Let laughed, and his rich, deep voice filled the warm cave. "Do not worry, Cia. I will explode many times tonight. We will do all the things you want to do and more." He'd been kneeling between her legs, but now, he raised his upper body and flexed his shoulders and arms to prove his strength.

Cia giggled and put out a hand to touch his upper arm, only to find it was as solid as a rock. She took his long fingers in hers and twined her fingers with his. "You are my mate."

Let smiled. "Yes. You are my mate."

"We will be mated for as long as Tec is in the sky."

"Yes, my mate."

Cia took his hand and rubbed his fingers on her tit. "Do you like this, my mate?"

Let's fingers trembled. "Oh, yes." The deep pink tip of her tit blossomed under his finger, and he gently pinched her hard nipple between thumb and forefinger. She moaned, and Let was moved to do it again.

Cia's body arched off the bearskin. "Fuck me," she begged in a tortured voice.

"Soon, my mate." Let continued to play with her tit with one hand, and with the other, he stroked her clit. Cia moaned and stuffed a fist in her mouth to cover the sound.

Let bent over and licked her other tit. She tasted of woman's flesh and smelled of flowers and honey.

His cock ached. He needed to explode. This was the longest he'd ever held off an eruption.

He took his cock in one hand and rubbed the head of it against her woman's place. "I will fuck you now, yes?"

Cia frowned and put her hand down to stop him. "Stop."

Let froze. "What? Do I hurt you?"

"No, but you will if you just push your cock in fast."

"Oh?"

"I am very tender, and you are very big. You must be gentle, my mate." She ran a soft finger down the length of his massive cock and pushed the hood back to expose his dark knob. "Take your fingers and open my womanhood, Let."

He did as she asked. He could not stop his hand from shaking as he opened her petals.

"Now," she directed. "Very slowly, ease your cock into my cunt."

He wasn't going to be able to stop the explosion. His cock touched the flower-petal lips of her opening, and he spewed man-juice all over her. His hips jerked, and his cock continued to spew like the volcano.

"I am sorry." Let dropped his chin to his heaving chest. "I am sorry."

Cia smiled, and Let's heart swelled in his body. "It is all right, my mate. You are excited."

Let nodded.

"Can you do it again?"

Let grinned. "Oh, yes." He wrapped his large hand around his cock. He was still stiff and large.

Cia grinned with him. "Now, my mate. Open my petals once more, and ease your cock slowly into me."

Let put his fingers on the lips to her womanhood and opened her. He bent forward and licked her clit. The hard little nub swelled under his tongue. He suckled until she was quivering all over.

"Let, please," she whimpered.

Let slid the head of his cock into her opening, and Cia began to weep.

"I am hurting you?"

"Nooo," she moaned. "More, Let. More!"

Let eased more of his massive cock into her cunt.

"Yes." She sighed. "Like it. Do it more."

He pushed slowly until the curls guarding his cock tangled with her woman's curls. "We are one," he groaned, dropping his head to her neck.

"Touch your mouth to mine," she ordered.

His mouth blended with hers, and she stuck her tongue into his mouth. Let drew back and stared into her eyes. "Why did you do that?"

"Gem taught me. It is called a tongue kiss. Do you like it?"

Let nodded and leaned in for another. When her lips met his, he arched his body into hers. Cia quivered and opened her legs wider, taking him deeper.

Their hips began to move in a dance as old as time, and soon, Let spewed his man-juice deep into her body. His cock was still moving when Let fell, his mouth on her breast. "Cia?"

"Yes?" She shifted her hips to accommodate his length and weight.

"I can't find the words…"

"I know."

"I have felt nothing like that before. It was better than killing the biggest animal in the forest. I am empty for the first time in my life."

He nuzzled her neck and sucked the skin. "I will rest for a few minutes, and we will do it again. And again?"

She laughed, and the sound echoed against his ear. "As much as you want, my mate."

"I want to fuck all night."

"Then we will," she agreed and groaned when he pulled his cock out of her slippery cunt.

* * * *

His massive cock eased out of her cunt and made a funny noise as it slipped free. Man-juice and woman's honey coated his cock, and the bearskin under their bodies was wet with it. Let couldn't seem to get enough of Cia. He had fucked her until she fell asleep while he continued to pump his juice into her cunt.

He watched her sleep, stroking a finger along her pink cheek. Soft. Her body was so soft and sweet. He liked the way the tips of her breasts turned into tiny pebbles when he sucked on them. He especially liked sucking on her clit. She was delicious all over.

Tec!

His cock was hard again. How could it be?

He tried to count the number of times he had fucked her on his fingers and ran out of fingers.

So many times? He should be empty by now, and yet he wasn't.

No wonder Cia was asleep.

Let drew her body close to his. Lying on her side, she faced the cave wall with her head on his shoulder. He curled behind her, lifting her upper leg, and slid his large, hard shaft between her slippery cunt lips.

Even half-asleep, Cia was willing and pliant.

Let put his free arm around her body and stroked her tits to hard peaks. Cia moaned and began to move with his body.

In and out, he rocked against her bottom.

When his explosion drew near, he pulled out and spewed his man-juice all over her rounded, firm flesh.

They had tasted, suckled, licked, and kissed each other everywhere until they knew each other's bodies and scents as well as they knew their own, and yet when Let inhaled and Cia's scent filled his body, his head felt light, and he was hungry for more of her.

Let still couldn't put into words his feelings for this woman.

All he knew was she was his and he was hers. He was happier than he'd ever been in his short life.

They were one. Mated for life.

Sighing, Let finally fell asleep, curled against Cia's warmth.

* * * *

"Time for your morning meal, my mate," Cia whispered in Let's ear.

Let rolled from his belly to his back, and Cia giggled when she realized he was hard and ready to fuck again. She had counted on her fingers the times he had taken her during their mating and had run out of fingers before she ran out of fucks. Let was going to be a wonderful mate. She would never need another man. Let would keep her more than satisfied.

"My mate." Let groaned and ran a large, dark hand down his smooth body. Curling his long fingers around his shaft, he pushed the protective hood out of the way. "Suck me, Cia."

She wrapped her hands around his and bent to take his swollen manhood into her mouth. She feathered her tongue across the tip, sipping at the drops of man-juice forming under her eager licking.

Let groaned and threw his head back, arching his body off the bearskin bedding. "Harder," he demanded in a strangled growl. Cia complied, sucking until her cheeks were tight against her teeth.

"Ahhh." Let howled as his man-juice filled her mouth and dripped onto his balls.

Cia cupped his balls, catching the man-juice and smearing it on her breasts while she continued to nurse his cock.

Let never seemed to lose stamina. He was insatiable, always starving for more, and Cia couldn't get enough of him.

"Now, me," she demanded, tugging at his cock. Let sat up and grabbed her around the waist. In less time than it took to form a smile, Cia found he had impaled her on his hard shaft.

She sighed and sank down until he was high and hard in her cunt. "I will come now," she groaned, wiggling her ass against his thighs.

"Come?"

Cia grinned and rubbed his nose with hers. "Yes. Come. Like you did…explode like the volcano."

"Oh. Come. I like the word. Come, my mate," he said, lifting his hips and forcing his cock higher in her body. "Come!"

"Touch my clit, and I will come for you, Let." He understood what she wanted and did as she asked. He placed against her and

stroked as she had taught him. Soon, she was trembling from head to toe. "More," she wailed. "More…harder…more…"

Moisture oozed out of her body to blend with his, and his slick, hot cock slammed in and out of her body. The sound of their bodies meeting filled the cave, echoing off the walls.

"Come, Cia," Let moaned. "Come…"

Ahhhh!

Cia was unsure who was coming. Was it she? Was it he? Was it both of them?

It did not matter. They were one.

* * * *

Cia had confided her plans to her friend Gem, so she was not surprised when later she found hot food outside the sleeping cave.

"Thank you, my sister," Cia whispered, picking up the bowls of hot meat and vegetables.

Her belly was empty, and Let had complained he could not fuck if he didn't get something to eat soon. That would never do. Cia planned to fuck until they were both dizzy and limp with exhaustion. Maybe two or three more passings of Tec might be enough to satisfy her hunger for her mate, and then he would only have to fuck her once or twice a passing of Tec.

* * * *

Gem left food outside the sleeping cave at regular intervals. Cia and Let only left their cave to visit the scat cave and bathe. They waited until the main cave was empty and the families were sleeping. Then they would slip out into the night to lounge in the heated pool and scrub each other with herbs and the foaming soap Gem made.

It was a wonderful time in Cia's life. Let was going to be a wonderful help-mate. He was large and hard and easily aroused. He seemed to care for her, but neither of them could find the words to express their feelings. They rubbed noses and touched lips often. When they weren't fucking, they would hold each other and whisper soft words of wanting and care.

They talked about what they would do when they had their own clan. Cia told Let she had been looking for a place for the clan and may have found something.

Soon, they would go look at the cave and see if it would work. There would not be many of them at first, but clans grew, so they needed a place that would be comfortable.

* * * *

Today was the day Cia decided. She would tell the dwellers the news. She was going to leave the clan and start her own clan family. Let had learned well and was also ready to help her lead a clan. He was strong, and with Og in the clan, they would be safe.

"Yes," she whispered. "It is time."

"What?" Let mumbled, his head buried under the sleeping skins.

Cia flipped the skins back and giggled. "Fuck me, Let, and I will tell you what I was talking about."

Let was more than willing to fuck her. He rolled to his back and clasped his hands around his cock. "I am ready, Cia. Are you?" he asked.

Cia licked her lips. Yes, he was ready. Baby-making juice formed and ran down his cock, making him slippery. She climbed on him and let his massive cock slide slowly inside her body.

Ah, yes. This was what she had waited for her whole life. Her beautiful, strong man.

Later, lying in Let's heavily muscled arms, Cia sighed.

"What is it, Cia?" Let asked.

"Today, we will tell the elders it is time for us to start our own clan. You know the shaman claimed such when I was born, and now, it is time. I will be leader. You will be my help-mate. You understand what it means, don't you, Let?"

Let nodded.

Cia breathed in his scent and buried her nose in his neck. She wound her fingers through the dark curls guarding his cock and tugged gently. "I don't think you are old enough to fully understand what is going to happen."

"I am eighteen summers old. How old do I have to be?"

Cia licked his skin. He tasted of sweat and spice. "It has been a very long time since anyone left the cave to start another clan.. There are things to be done before we can leave."

Let stroked Cia's long hair and took a deep breath. "Things?"

Cia remained silent.

"What things?" Let asked.

"You will be not be happy when you hear, but it must be done before we can leave. Even though the shaman proclaimed me a leader,

I still must prove to the elders I am strong enough to leave and rule on my own."

Cia's hand moved from his man fur to stroke his belly. "Your skin is so smooth. I could touch you all day."

"Yes, but if you do, I will have to fuck you all day."

"Is that a bad thing?" Cia asked with a laugh.

Let laughed along with her. "No. I want to fuck you again. But first you must tell me what is worrying you."

"I don't want to, but you are now my mate, so I will."

Let put a heavy hand on Cia's teat and softly squeezed. "Tell me."

"In order to leave, I must prove I am strong, brave, and able to lead."

"Yes, you said so, but what does it mean?"

"I must leave the cave on my own and hunt the large, furry beast with the huge teeth. I must bring it down on my own, bring it home, and tan the hide." She sighed and wiggled against him, finding comfort with her head on his broad shoulder.

"If the animal is not large enough or the hide is not tanned correctly, then they may either not let me leave or force me to go hunting again. The worst thing would be if the elders decide they won't let me go unless I fight at least two of them to prove I can be strong as a man. I must be strong and swift as the best hunter, stronger than the elders. Brave and strong."

"If you have to fight them, what happens?"

"If the elders win, they will show their power by fucking me while you watch. They will want to humiliate me."

Cia had her hand on Let's chest, and she felt his heart leap at her words. She waited for him to forbid her.

"Go on," was all he said. He left unsaid his fear and anger. Being a clansman was a hard life. Nothing came easy to men and women alike.

"I must hunt alone. If I do not return, then I have gone to live with Tec. If I return with what they want, then they will decide if I am strong enough, or they might demand I fuck two of the clansmen of my choice to prove beyond doubt how strong and brave I am."

"If they demand their way with me—and they might—then my mate must take me after they are done. If you refuse, it will prove I have made a fool of you, and you can leave me to pick a new mate. If you still want me after the two men are finished with me, my mate will have to fuck me in front of the cave-dwellers to prove he believes in my strength and bravery. Then and only then can I leave and start a new clan."

Let sighed. "I don't care how many men fuck you, my Cia. I will always want you. You are mine and mine alone. No one will take your heart, for it is mine."

Cia took his hand and placed it over her breast. "Feel that? It beats only for you."

"Yes. I know."

"While I waited for you to become a man, I pleasured many men, and you watched me. Knowing I was with other men does not seem to bother you. You still want me. This will be no different. They will never have my heart, only my cunt."

"I know. I do not care about the fucking. I do not like them sending you out alone to find and kill the large, furry animal. I have seen the furry beast kill a man with one stomp of its foot. I do not want you to die to prove you are strong."

She nuzzled his neck and licked him once more. "You are a good mate. Better even than Og. You are my heart. I am afraid to hunt the furry one, but if I know you are waiting for my return, I can do what is demanded of me, Let. You make me brave and strong."

* * * *

Much later, they ate their evening meal and cleaned up the cave. Cia took Let's large hand in hers, and they walked to the center fire of the main cave. Cia held Let's hand in the air.

"Behold my mate. Let is mine for all time."

The older dwellers moved their hands in a song of joy while the younger dwellers used their voices to make a noise they called singing. The youngest girl, Lia, had a voice as sweet as the wind on a summer day. She was the one who had made up the song. The others followed her lead, blending their voices into one.

When the song was over, Cia let go of Let's hand and raised both of hers toward the curved ceiling of the cave.

"The time has come for me to be leader of my own clan. It is my right to ask for leadership, and it is time for Let and me to go out on our own."

Lia came to stand next to Cia and signed for the old dwellers who did not understand the words. There were many gasps.

The elders signed together a resounding, "*No.*"

Cia did not let them dissuade her from her decision. She repeated her declaration in a louder voice. "I want to be leader of my own clan. It is my right. The shaman proclaimed it on my date of birth."

The eldest of the elders, Tre, one of the wisest men of the elders, stepped forward, shaking his head. "No one has ever left us before. Do you know what trial you must go through to become head of a clan?" Cia nodded. "Yes, Old One, I understand, and I am ready." Calling an elder "Old One" was not disrespectful. It was a name of high honor among the elders.

Tre turned and stared at the other elders. They signed furiously back and forth for what seemed like forever. Cia held onto Let's hand and felt his strength flow from his body to hers.

Gem signed as Tre spoke. "It is our decision, Cia, that you will hunt the large, furry animal. Kill it and bring it back here with no help. When that is done, we will again discuss your wishes for a clan of your own."

Cia signed her thanks to the elders.

Tre continued to speak. "You know if we are not satisfied, you must pick two of the clansmen to fuck. We must see how strong and brave you are. Bring us the largest furry animal you can find, and we will decide after the hunt if you must fuck two men."

Let stirred next to Cia. "Silent," she whispered to him. "Do not argue."

"But—" he mumbled.

"No. It is all as I warned you. Be silent, or they will tie you up until I return." Cia smiled and said, "Good, we agree, Old One. I leave tomorrow at the rising of Tec and will return with my prize—the furry beast."

Cia's mother had been silent, sitting at her fire pit. She stood and signed. "Go with Tec, my daughter. You will be leader of your own clan soon."

Cia's father stood and pulled his mate's hand. "*Sit down, woman,*" he signed.

Her mother yanked her arm free and gathered Sin closed to her breast. She stood beside Cia and raised her hand in the air. "This is my daughter. She will be leader." She turned to Cia and put her hand on Cia's shoulder. "Go with Tec. Be strong. I will feed and care for Let while you are gone."

"Mother," Cia gasped. "You can speak?"

Her mother nodded. "It does not make your father happy, but I learned to speak when you were a child. I couldn't hold my mouth closed any longer. Bend down," she ordered her daughter.

Cia bent down, and Fa kissed her forehead. "Be safe."

"Thank you, Mother. I will be very careful." She kissed her mother's forehead. "Thank you for taking care of Let. Watch him so he does not follow. For if he follows, the others may harm him."

"I will watch him like the eagle who lives on the top of the cliffs."

* * * *

After a celebratory dinner served by all the clanswomen, Let and Cia went to their sleeping cave. Of course they could not leave without a lot of teasing, both in sign language and by word. Everyone was laughing and happy for the lovers, even though they knew that tomorrow, all could change in an instant.

Because of the lives they led, death was a fact of life. At any moment, a tiger could steal a child or a hairy mammoth could stomp a man or child. A snake could slither into the cave and eat a baby before anyone was aware of the intruder. Spiders were poisonous, and even the bats who lived in the caves were dangerous. They ate a lot of bugs, but sometimes, a sick bat would bite a dweller, and he would die of a horrible sickness.

It was a terrifying way to live.

Most dwellers lived moment to moment, laughing and loving as much as they could because tomorrow, death might be at the door.

Let was not worried about their sleeping cave. He kept it spotless for his mate. He swept every day and shook out the sleeping skins every rising of Tec.

Let and Cia stopped at the scat caves and then met in the narrow walkway. "Do you want to swim tonight in the hot pool?" Cia asked. Let agreed it would be nice. They stopped at their sleeping cave and got rabbit fur to dry off with and clean aprons to wear back—although Cia didn't plan for the aprons to stay on long once they returned.

The pool was empty, the night silent. Tec's sons had lit their fires in the sky. The breeze was warm and pleasant. The lovers kissed and slid into the pool. Cia placed herself on Let's lap, close to his cock but not too close. She wasn't ready to fuck yet. She had something to say to her mate, and her heart told her it was important.

"Let?"

"Mmm." He tried to pull her closer, but Cia put a hand on his smooth chest.

"I have so many things I want to say to you, but I'm not sure how to say them. There are so many new words every day, and I want to use them all. Gem and I made up a new word yesterday, and I think this night is the time to tell you."

Let's brows furrowed. Cia smiled and kissed the furrows away.

"I am afraid, Cia. Must you go?"

"Yes. If I want to be clan leader, I have to go." She pushed her fingers through his dark, tightly curled hair and brought his face to hers. They rubbed noses and kissed. "I will not be gone long. I know where the hairy mammoth lives. I will be home in seven settings of Tec. Have faith in me, my mate, for I love you and will not leave you."

"Love? What is love?"

"Love is the funny feeling we get when we are together. The way we do not want to be parted. It is also the fear you feel for me and I feel for you. Fear you will be gone forever. Fear, fucking, and other feelings make love have meaning."

Let nodded and smiled. His white teeth gleamed brightly. "Then that means I love you, Cia."

She moved closer to his body and gave him a teasing smile. "Really?"

"Yes."

"How much?"

"I don't know, but I think I can show you." He'd been sitting on a natural ledge of rock. He knew Cia was squatting on the same ledge. He lifted her and put her over his cock. "I want you more than ever before. Please, Cia, fuck me. Fuck me hard."

She straddled his enormous cock and slid down his shaft until he was touching her womb. "Aahh," she moaned. "Yes...yes. You are my lover."

He pushed as far inside her as he possible could and then lifted her and slid her back down slowly. "Does it feel good, Cia?"

"Oh, Tec. You are touching my heart, Let. I love you."

That night, their lovemaking was hot and furious in the pool. Eventually, they got out, dried off, and went back to their sleeping cave, where they made slow, sweet love until they fell asleep still connected, still one with the other.

* * * *

She was gone. Let shuffled through the skins but could not find his mate anywhere. He searched the cave. Her spear and club were gone, as was her backpack and water holder.

Cia had left without saying goodbye. She would be back. He could feel it in his heart, and his heart was heavy with fear and love. Let whispered a short prayer to Tec for her safe return.

He cleaned and neatened the cave and went looking for Fa. She had promised to take care of him while his mate was hunting the beast. Let was hungry enough to eat a whole antelope.

"Glory to Tec," Let greeted Fa. He rubbed his belly. "I am hungry. Is there food, good woman?"

"Glory to Tec," she answered and motioned for him to be seated on the fur rug next to the fire. "I have brown brew, antelope stew, and flat bread."

Let smiled. "I am very hungry."

Fa served him a large bowl of hot stew, a smaller bowl of brown brew, and a huge piece of flat bread.

Flat bread was something the women of the tribe had been experimenting with in recent passings of Tec. They used dried corn ground to a fine powder and added water. When it was mixed, they rolled and kneaded the mixture in more dried powder until it was stiff. They broke off pieces and patted them flat and draped the pieces over hot rocks. The result was tasty, especially when filled with the hot stew.

One of the women had found other dried grains, and they ground the grains using the same method as the corn. The breads were very good, but once in a while, a small piece of rock would be inside the bread. Many had broken a tooth. The pain was bad, but the food was worth the discomfort.

Let

The women tried to be careful when they mixed the bread to make sure the hot rocks were clean and clear of sand.

"Thank you, woman. I am full."

Fa signed her happiness and warned him not to disappear.

Let wandered the cave for what seemed like a lifetime, and then he grabbed his spear and club and headed for the cave door.

Tre was standing in his way. "Where you go?"

"Hunting." Let shook his spear to prove his point.

"Not alone. I will go with you."

Let was not happy but had suspected Tre would not leave him alone today. It didn't matter. He had talked to Og and begged him to stay out of sight. All Let wanted Og to do was make sure Cia would not get injured. Og had promised he would do nothing to interfere unless he had to save her. Let had also asked Og not to tell Gem. Og had agreed only because he, too, did not want his brother-friend's mate to be injured.

Let and Tre headed out of the cave and climbed the rock wall to the cliffs above their cave Many tasty flying animals lived in the cliffs. It was not easy to bring them down with a spear, but Let was an expert with stone throwing and within a short time brought down two plump flying things. Cia called them birds. Let didn't care what they were called, he just thought they tasted good roasted over the home fire.

He and Tre continued to hunt silently while Let prayed to Tec to keep his beautiful Cia safe.

* * * *

Cia set out before Tec had climbed over the cliff. The sky was still dark, but the fires of Tec's sons were disappearing one by one. She grasped her spear in one hand and her club in the other. Her water bladder and the pack with food in it dug into her shoulder. They bounced against her back and annoyed her greatly.

She had kissed Let goodbye before she left, but she had worn him out and he hadn't stirred. He had continued to sleep like a baby. She couldn't bring herself to wake him. He was so beautiful lying there with a soft smile on his full lips. His eyes were closed, but she remembered how his deep, dark eyes sparkled when he was happy and how she could read sadness in them when he was worried. He'd been very worried when he had finally fallen asleep.

It was chilly and damp. Wet, tall grasses slapped against her and made her feel chilly all the way through her body. When Tec reached over the cliffs, it would warm up, and soon, she would be wishing it was night again.

Cia set a steady pace and covered ground swiftly. So far, she had seen no sign of the massive, hairy mammoth. She slipped through an opening in a wall of rock and ended up in a new valley. She stood silently. Nose in the air, Cia took a deep breath. The animal she searched for was here somewhere.

This valley was full of trees, tall bushes, and high grasses. Everything was very green. Not only did she smell the filthy animal, she could also smell water. She walked silently through the tall grasses, the scent of water and mammoth becoming stronger and stronger.

The moment she spied the water through the trees, she also saw the beast. It was much larger than she remembered. Of course, the last time she'd seen one, she had been on a cliff quite far from the animal. Now, she was within a tree-length of the mammoth, and it was gigantic.

She was going to have to stab it in the throat. It was the only way to get it down. She'd listened to the men around the fire and had learned it was the only way to bring down a mammoth.

She crept silently through the grass. She was well trained in the hunt. Nothing stirred the foliage. What little breeze there was blew past the beast toward her. As long as the wind stayed in that direction, she would be safe, for the animal would not catch her scent.

Silent moments passed. Cia crept forward slowly, staying low to the ground. It seemed to take forever, but when she looked up, she was startled to find she was under the huge head and horns of the beast.

She had to do this right, or she would be dead. She took a deep breath and let it out. She clutched the spear so tight her fingers ached. With one mighty upward shove, she speared the hairy beast in the throat. The polished, sharpened obsidian slid smoothly into the animal, but the blade struck something in its neck, and the spear slipped sideways, taking Cia with it.

The mammoth screamed and lifted a giant front foot. The next thing Cia knew, she was flying backward. Her body arched over grass and bushes before she landed with a horrible thump and rolled over several times.

Oh, Tec. She was hurt. Badly.

She had ended up lying on her left arm in a bed of sharp rocks. She'd seen enough injuries to other hunters to know she was seriously injured. Her left arm wouldn't move without the help of her free one. Her stomach and side hurt, and one leg was twisted strangely.

The animal screamed once again, and Cia covered her head with her good arm. She was going to die. "I love you, Let," she whispered before the world went dark.

* * * *

Og rushed past Cia before the beast could step on her, and with his hunting shaft held firmly between his hands, he killed the animal with one blow. He jumped back when the beast fell to the ground with a terrible rumble.

Now, he had a problem—how to get Cia back to the cave and the beast also. He built a fire, made a thick mat of grass, and picked up Cia with great care. He laid her on the grass bed. There wasn't much he could do for her injuries until he'd started skinning the dead beast.

He found two slender trees, cut them down with his obsidian knife, and trimmed off the leaves. Next, he took his knife and made a slash as long as he was tall from the animal's cock to below its front legs. With practiced, hurried strokes, he skinned the animal around the middle. He cut long, thin strips of skin and tied each end to the two trees. He then sliced a large piece of the skin to fit over the travois, poked holes in it, and tied it to the trees.

He chopped off hunks of meat and put them to cook over the fire using slim, green branches to keep the meat from falling in the fire. While the meat cooked, Cia moaned but did not cry. She was a brave woman. Let would be very proud of her.

Og made a second travois and attached it to the first with strips of animal skin. He hacked huge hunks of meat off the animal and piled them on the second travois until it was so heavy he wasn't sure he could move it. Last he slipped his knife carefully around the massive curved tusks, and small fuzzy ears and piled them on top of the heap of meat. He tied it securely.

He heated water, put some cooked meat in it, and fed it to Cia. She only moaned but drank the life-giving broth. Og fed her through the night and tried to keep her comfortable. Sometimes, she cried out for Let, but most of the time she simply stared at the sky with tears in her eyes.

Og knew why she cried and continued to assure her the elders would never know he had been the one to drive in the death blow. Cia deserved the kill. Her shaft had struck the animal correctly, and eventually it would have bled to death, but Og hadn't had time to wait for it to die. He'd had to get Cia out of the way.

Cia sent Og to find a certain tree and strip the bark. He brought it back, boiled it, and gave the brew to her to drink. It seemed to ease her pain, and before she dropped off to sleep, she asked him to be sure to brew enough for the trip back to the cave.

At the dawning of Tec, Og made sure Cia was as comfortable as he could make her. He secured her to the first travois and lifted the end. His muscles bulged and quivered, but once he got the two sleds moving, it became easier. He headed toward the opening to their valley. He would not be able to get her through the narrow opening, but he could call for help. Let would be waiting for the call. So would the rest of the clan. It wouldn't take long for the men to get her back to her mother's home fire.

Cia was silent. Og became frightened. If she went to join Tec in the sky, Let would never forgive him, and neither would Og's mate, Gem. He checked, and she was asleep. The bark brew was helping her rest. Og stopped once more to give Cia more of the sleeping brew. He drank deeply from his water bladder and set off again toward the opening that marked their valley.

* * * *

The tribe was more than willing to believe Og's story of coming upon the injured Cia after she had killed the mighty beast. Let waited until he was alone with Og to find out the truth and to thank his brother-friend for saving his mate's life.

"I have talked to her mother, and she said Cia will recover soon. Most of her injuries are minor. Her leg is broken, and her arm is full of rocks and dirt. Fa has scrubbed the wounds with a mixture Gem made, and they have put a paste of healing herbs on all the cuts. Fa bound Cia around the middle to ease her pain and gave her some other herbs to drink. Cia will sleep for a long time," Let explained to Og.

"I have no words to tell you how glad I am you were there to save my mate."

"Do not worry, Let. We are brother-friends. You would do the same for me, yes?"

"Yes."

"Go to your mate and sit with her. Lie with her and keep her warm. Whisper words of love to her, and she will be well very soon."

Let nodded, looking toward his mate who lay so silent and still at her mother's home fire.

"Go, my brother-friend. Soon, she will need your big cock to keep her company."

Let punched Og in the upper arm and laughed. "I hope so, because I miss her hot cunt wrapped around me."

Og put an understanding hand on Let's shoulder. They had been trying to keep their fear from showing, but now, Og said, "She will need you, Let. She is frightened and hurt. She's afraid she will not be made head of her own clan. You must make her believe."

* * * *

Let spent every hour he was allowed to with his mate, and soon, Cia was alert and talking. Her pain was better thanks to Gem and Fa. She was healing on the outside, but Let knew she still was bothered by something.

One night, when the cave was silent, except for a few cracklings of branches in fire pits and snorts of the sleeping men, Let curled up next to Cia. "I love you, my mate."

"Oh, Let," she whispered. "I love you."

"You are so sad. Is it because of me?"

"Only because you do not fuck me anymore. Am I ugly? Are you ashamed because I did not kill the beast with one blow?"

Let blew in her ear, and Cia shivered. "Mmm. Good."

"I have been forbidden to fuck you by your mother. She said I would hurt you."

Cia snuggled closer to her mate. Her arm was healed and no longer hurt. Her leg was still strapped between several knee-length, small branches Let had shaved until they were smooth as obsidian. Fa said they would release her leg in a few more passings of Tec. "I only hurt because you do not fuck me."

She smoothed her hand along his burnished back, enjoying the play of muscles under skin. He was so beautiful, and she had missed his body next to hers. Even more, she missed the closeness she felt in her heart when they fucked.

"Let, fuck me?"

"I have been thinking..."

"No fucking?"

Let chuckled quietly. "No. I have thought of new words while you have been hurt."

"Tell me."

"We do not fuck."

Tears welled up in her eyes. Warrior women did not let their eyes water, but she couldn't stop it. "Never?"

"Never."

Cia's body started to shake, and the tears ran like rain down her face.

Let held her closer. "No. We will make love. Making love is better than fucking. It is...special."

"It is?"

His large hand cupped her breast. "It is very special. Do you want me to show you?"

Cia wiped away her tears. "Oh, yes. I think I understand. We make love to each other because we love each other?"

Let rubbed her nose and kissed her very softly. "Yes. We will make love."

Cia wished the night would never end. Let kissed her body from her toes to her forehead and then down her back to her feet. He kissed her in places she had never been kissed before. He licked her nipples until she was begging for his cock, but he put her hands over her head and stilled her begging with more kisses.

He licked her cunt and sucked the hard nub of her clit into his mouth. Her body arched off the bearskin they lay on, and she whimpered. It hurt her leg, but she didn't care. All she wanted was her mate inside her body. Finally, he eased his large cock into her, and for the first time in days, she felt soothed and loved.

"Enough," Let said after they had exploded. "You need to rest. I'm sure making love has hurt your leg. Rest. We will do it again tomorrow."

She wrapped her arms around his upper body and pulled him up to kiss him. "I love you, Let. Love me now? I need your cock inside me."

"Soon." Let smoothed her hair off her face and put his hands on both sides of her cheeks. "You are mine. I love you. I'm sorry you were hurt and I was not there."

"But you sent Og. You did the right thing, Let. You saved my life."

She opened her legs, offering herself to him. He knelt between her knees and stroked the insides of her legs. "You are so soft. So warm. So beautiful."

"Please, Let. Please come into me."

Let grasped his large cock in both his hands and eased himself into her. He put his mouth over hers when she opened her mouth to scream her excitement.

Let was large and heavily muscled. Without losing his place deep inside her, he sat up, bringing her with him until she was straddling his lap. He'd even managed the maneuver without hurting her leg. He continued to kiss her. He wrapped his long-fingered hands around her waist so he could lift her and slide her up and down on his rock-hard shaft. Many times, he lifted her high enough to suckle her nipples, and every time, her internal muscles tightened around his hot, dark pole. "You will be mine. My Cia. My love," he exclaimed.

"Yes, yes, yes. More, Let. More." Her insides were trembling, and her explosion was near. She bit her lip to keep from screaming when his hand slipped between them and rubbed her clit.

They both shuddered and shook as they fell together into the heat of Tec.

A short time later, Let gathered her close to his body, and they drifted off to sleep. Before she dozed off, Cia grinned. Her mother was not going to be happy to find them together in the morning. She didn't think Cia was well enough to be with her mate. For once, Fa was wrong.

* * * *

"I have called you all together," Cia said to the members of their cave. "It has taken me a long time to recover from my injuries, but I am now strong, and it is time for me to start my own tribe. My mate, Let, and I are ready to go out on our own. I am wondering if there are any of you who want to come with us?"

Lia stood to the side and signed Cia's words for the old people.

Many of the older men frowned. They did not like change. Their mates had no say in the matter, so they sat silently in the background.

Og turned to his mate and smiled. Gem nodded. "We will," Og said loudly. He held up his spear so there was no doubt who was speaking.

"Thank you, my friend-brother," Let said.

"Any others?" Cia asked.

Two or three more spears were raised. Most were young couples who were ready to leave the boundaries set by the old ones.

"Good," Cia said, smiling at them all. "Let and I welcome you into our clan. Come join us by our fire pit, and we will talk."

Once everyone was seated, Cia served their guests hot brown brew in rock bowls and then seated herself in front of the fire.

"Have you found a cave yet?" Og asked.

"Let and I have been looking. We have found something in the next valley. The cave is not perfect, but it will work after we all do some digging and cleaning. It will be ready before the cold white begins to cover the land, but we must work hard together. There will be wood to bring in to dry and the black rocks of coal." She sipped from her cup.

"We will all help," the new clan agreed in one voice.

Mac held his mate Wen's hand and said, "The men can find the wood and cut it while the women gather the coal. We will all dig out our own sheltering cove in the main cave. The work will go fast if we work together."

The group nodded.

"Let and I will hunt for food and meat. Our mates can dry what we gather and fill the food cove with as much as we will need for the cold time," Og added.

Cia and Gem agreed.

"It will be very hard work," Cia said, wringing her hands. "Are you sure you want to do this? Because unless we work together, we will freeze or starve."

Mac held up a hand. "We understand our lives depend on how hard we must work. It can be done."

Again, the new clan nodded.

"Wait," Tog spoke from his seat on the highest rock ledge.

Silence reigned.

Cia knew Tog was going to stop them before the new clan could even try to leave the cave.

Let took her hand. "It will be all right," he assured Cia in a whisper.

She smiled. "I love you." He stared in her eyes and smiled.

"You know the rules for leaving the cave," Tog growled.

Cia nodded and remained silent. If the elders were happy with her kill of the hairy mammoth, Tog would let them leave without too much anger, but if they were not happy, she would be forced to fight the strongest, largest man in the cave using her obsidian knife as her only weapon. It would be her last chance to prove how strong and brave she was or die trying.

"Tonight, the elders will make their final decision." Tog's fierce face usually frightened even the bravest of men, but Cia was not intimidated. The fact that he seldom used his voice made him even more intimidating. She stared hard into his eyes. Tog would never know the fear in her heart.

"Leave us," Tog demanded. "We will call you back when we have an answer."

Let took Cia's hand and led her out of the cave. Running down the trail, Let took Cia to their favorite pool. "A swim and some fucking will help to make you forget what is going on in the cave, my mate," Let said and helped Cia loosen her leather skirt. He quickly stripped off his and jumped in the warm water. He held up his arms to catch her.

Cia laughed and jumped. He pretended to drop her, but he caught her and held her tight against his body.

"I can feel your cock." Cia smiled and reached between them to caress his shaft and balls.

"Enough, woman. I will fuck you in a few minutes. First, I want to rub you all over with the oils Gem made for you."

The rock bowls were kept near the edge of the pool with a flat piece of rock on top to keep out the water that sometimes fell from the sky.

Someone had been there before them, and there were petals of flowers floating on the water, filling the heated air with the same scent as the oils Let would be using.

He put Cia on a rock bench and got out of the pool. He spread a large, soft skin on the ground and gestured for her to get out and join him. She scrambled up the rock steps.

"Lay down, my love," Let said with gentle authority. She did as he'd suggested, and when she was settled on her belly with her arms under her chin, Let poured more oil over her back and arms. His large hands began to move sensuously over her back and shoulders. Then he rubbed her arms gently. He was very conscious of his size and was careful not to injure her.

Soon, he had her as relaxed as a new cave cat across a little girl's lap. He poured more oil on her bottom and thighs and continued to work the oil into her skin. He massaged her bottom, and when she raised her butt to keep his large hands in contact with her body, he put an oily finger in her anus and finger-fucked her until she was screaming for more.

He flipped her over and teased her nipples with his tongue. He worked his finger into her cunt and made love to her with his fingers, and then when she couldn't stand the suspense any longer, he placed his mouth where his fingers had been and sucked her clit until it was long and hard.

She was wet and ready for him when he entered her, and they began the rhythm of the dance of love—a dance as old as time.

They were so anxious for each other it didn't take long for Cia to reach her dreamworld, and Let followed soon thereafter.

They rested for a short time, and then Let lowered Cia into the pool. They made love once more before Let rubbed her dry and helped her into her leather apron. It was harder to get Let dressed because Cia couldn't keep her hands off his cock. Eventually, he set her high on a rock and got dressed without her help.

They held hands and walked back to cave, taking their time. Outside of the cave, Let gave her a deep, spine-tingling kiss. "Remember, if they will not let us start our own clan, we will wait until Tog is gone to live with Tec, and then we will try again. I have no fear. You will be leader."

She rubbed his nose and whispered, "I wish this night was over, my mate."

"It will be soon. And when it is over, you will be leader."

His movements had been slow and soothing. He kissed her and smoothed his hands up and down her body. "You will be leader."

* * * *

"I love you," she whispered.

"I love you," he answered. "Are you ready?"

She nodded. She took Let's hand in hers and kissed his full, warm lips. "I am ready."

"I will be here for you, my mate. Do not be afraid. Do not be ashamed if we must stay. We will live here without shame."

"Thank you, my mate."

"Tog." Let raised his voice so he could be heard above the noise. "Cia is ready for the elders' decision."

"Come forward, girl, and stand in the center." Tog ordered.

Cia strode bravely where Tog pointed and straightened her spine. No man was going to make her cower. The silence was terrifying, but Cia did not flinch.

Tog stood and opened his arms wide. "The elders were not happy when you asked to become leader of your own clan. I agreed with them until you were able to kill the mammoth without getting killed yourself."

She opened her mouth to speak, and Tog gestured for her to remain silent.

"Yes, you were injured, but many warriors have been injured when hunting. It is part of our life. You were very brave, Cia. You brought down a huge beast. Og was able to gather much meat, and when the men went back, they were able to bring home even more meat. The women have soaked enough meat in brine to last many moons."

Cia dropped her head and stared at the floor. So far, only Og and Let knew the truth, and both men had sworn allegiance to Cia. They would never tell.

"One of the elders suggested you should perhaps see how many men you can fuck, but..."

Cia shuddered. *No. Please. No.*

Tog hadn't see her shudder. He continued speaking. "I have told them it is not necessary. You are a strong, brave woman and do not need to prove your strength yet again."

Cia took a deep breath.

"We have decided you may take those who want to leave and begin your own clan. We have decided to share the salted meat of the mammoth, and the young men will help you load a travois. Go with Tec."

Cia lowered her head. "Thank you."

* * * *

Cia no longer felt fear. She was going to be leader of her own clan. She was happy. She wanted to laugh and cry at the same time.

She thanked Tec many times she had not had to fuck or fight with any of the elders. The only man she wanted was the man kissing her at this moment. All she wanted was the man above her. Let knew her body like his own, and soon, he had her purring and happy against him. Rubbing her teats against his chest wall, Cia murmured his name.

"Fuck me, Let," she whimpered, tugging at the fingers he had buried in her cunt.

"Not yet, Cia," he groaned. "Soon, my mate. Soon." His fingers reached higher inside her body, and Cia cried out as she reached her climax.

"Yes, oh…yes, my love. More," she begged, opening her legs wide for him.

Let knelt between her legs and touched the knob of his cock against her cunt lips. "I will be very slow. You will like it. Yes?" He pushed his cock into her.

"Ahhh." Cia groaned. "That is good. More, Let. Give me more…"

Let slowly eased his cock into her cunt until he was seated all the way to his balls inside her.

"I love you, Let," she whispered.

As he began pumping his hips, Let cried out his love for Cia.

Cia and Let exploded at the same time, collapsing in a human heap on the pile of bearskins, and she immediately fell asleep in Let's embrace.

* * * *

"Wake up, my Cia." Let shook Cia's slender shoulder.

She stretched and yawned, opening her eyes to stare at her lover. "Is it over, my mate?"

Let grinned. "It is over, and you are now free to be leader. You were very strong and brave."

Cia sighed. "Was I brave?"

"Very."

"Good. It was not something I want to go through again."

"You will never have to prove anything. You are leader of your own clan. And from now until the end of time, you will be mine."

"Thank you for being with me. I was afraid you would not want me if I was forbidden my own clan."

Let smiled and pulled her into his arms. "I will always want you, Cia. I love you."

"For all time?"

"For all time."

THE END

SIREN PUBLISHING *Allure*

SIN

CHERIE DENIS
Caveman Love

SIN

Caveman Love 3

CHERIE DENIS
Copyright © 2011

His foot slipped on the shale, and a piece flew out, barely missing his brother-friend, Lef. "Sorry," Sin mumbled, scrabbling for a better finger hold. Another rock shot out from under his foot.

Lef grumbled, "Slow down, Sin. You are getting dirt in my eyes."

"We are late. We must hurry, or we will not get back to the cave before Tec leaves the sky."

"It is your fault we are late," Lef was quick to remind Sin. "If you had not wanted to stop and watch Em and Ria bathe, we would have had lots of time."

Sin shrugged his shoulders. "You are right, my brother. I will not argue with you since it is the truth." He turned and stared down at Lef. "Admit it, my friend. You wanted to watch them also."

Lef's full lips curved in a broad grin. "Yes. You are right. It was worth wasting time to watch them. They are both so beautiful."

Sin dug his long, thin fingers into the loose rock and pulled himself up to the next outcrop. Here, it was hotter, and the wind tore at his hair. He rubbed his face on his bare shoulder. The sweat rolling down his forehead burned his eyes and made it almost impossible to see.

Sin pushed with his bare feet and in moments was seated on a narrow ledge. "Hurry up, Lef." Sin ran his dirty fingers through his hair, brushing it back.

Lef's grinning face appeared over the edge.

Sin and Lef had grown up together, and Sin could count on one hand the times Lef had frowned. His friend was almost always in a good mood. Ria had told Sin once in secret she thought Lef was the handsomest warrior in their clan. Sin wasn't so sure he agreed, but he would admit his friend was nice to look at.

"Move over, my brother," Lef ordered, pulling himself up to plant his ass on the ledge next to Sin. "How much longer?"

"You keep asking, and I will leave you behind," Sin grumbled. He peered over his shoulder. "We are almost there. If we hurry, we will be at the top and be home before dark."

Lef carried their water in a pouch slung over his neck. He turned the strap, pulled the plug of grass out of the pouch, took a hearty drink, and handed it to his brother-friend. "Drink, my friend, and then we will move on toward the top."

Under their bottoms, the earth heaved and moaned. Sin's eyebrows shot up, as did Lef's. "We must hurry. Pot is growing angrier with each passing of Tec, the sun god."

Lef took a second drink of the cool, nearly tasteless water, put the grass plug back in the top, and stood. He draped the strap of the water pouch over his shoulder and pushed it around until it rested comfortably at his back. "I am ready. Lead on, my brother."

Sin took the hand Lef offered and let his friend pull him to his feet. The ground wobbled and sighed. It was not a good sign. The signs had been growing worse by the day, and this was the third trip up the side of Pot the two had made in the past five passings of Tec.

Sin's sister, Cia, leader of their clan, was worried. The great volcano, Pot, was going to explode one day soon, and she was making plans to move the dwellers to a new location. Cia and her mate, Let, Lef's older brother, had been searching far and wide for a new cave that would not be in the path of Pot's anger.

This was not the first time the volcano had erupted, and the dwellers knew well what destruction Pot could leave after an explosion. The dwellers were nervous, edgy, and anxious to be on their way. Cia insisted Sin and Lef, being the most agile of the dwellers, be the ones to climb to the top of Pot and see how large the dome inside had grown. Knowing the size would give Cia an idea how much time they had left before the eruption.

Pot grumbled, and Sin shuddered. He wished they had not spent so long watching Em and Ria bathing, but still he felt it had been worth the lost time. He had been keeping track of the moons rising and waning, waiting anxiously as Em grew into full womanhood. Now, by counting the passings of Tec on his fingers, he knew Em was finally of age. . This was her eighteenth summer.

Cia had promised Em's mother that Sin would not mate with her lovely daughter until she was old enough. Sin was getting tired of waiting especially now that Em was old enough. Just the thought of Em's growing teats and dark pink nipples made him hard and aching. Lef seemed to be having the same problem. He desired to mate with Ria, a pretty, small, dark-haired girl who was the same age as Em.

The two girls had grown up together as he and Lef had. They were more like sisters than friends. Their looks were similar, yet different. Where Em's face was round and soft, Ria's was more square and hard. Their hair was dark and long, hanging down their backs to the creases of high, firm buttocks. The rest of their bodies were hairless, except for the small amount of fur guarding the woman's place. The place the men called a cunt.

Em's teats—"breasts," his sister Cia had informed him—were heavy and full, almost as large as Cia's. Her body was a woman's body, and Sin hungered for her. Ria had small teats, but Lef said he liked small teats because they would fit in his mouth and hands better.

Almost nineteen summers, the young men were feeling omnipotent as they reached their full manhood. Both were blessed with large, firm cocks, and the older women of the cave often made a point of offering to teach them what they needed to know to satisfy a mate. So far Sin had managed to elude their advances, but Lef had taken advantage of the offer a time or two, and said he had no words to describe how good fucking made him feel.

Lef's stories only made Sin more anxious to slip his cock into Em's hot cunt.

Sin knew he was a very lucky man to have a sister like Cia, who was smart and willing to teach the dwellers the words needed to talk to friends and fellow men. Theirs was a cave inhabited by many young and bright people. Cia was the one who had given him most of the words he had for talking and thinking about Em. Some words he and Lef had made up, so when it came to Em and Ria, Sin and Lef did not lack for ways to discuss them.

The earth rumbled and grumbled as the young men clambered toward the summit of Pot. Dark gray, hot smoke billowed out of Pot, and ash landed on their heads and shoulders, scalding their skin. It was much worse today than it had been on any other day previously. Sin's insides quivered. Fear crept under his skin like a worm eating at his gut.

The heat grew more and more unbearable as they scrambled closer to the summit. "I am beginning to worry, Lef. Pot is grumbling more than usual." Sin pulled himself up the last few feet and, finding a firm spot, planted his broad, bare feet. Lef stopped next to him, and they crept as close as possible to the edge of the crater.

Peering over the rocks, they both gasped and jumped back. Indescribable heat boiled up and surrounded them, nearly burning their skin and singeing the hair in their noses.

Their eyes burned, and sweat ran off their bodies.

What they had seen would be with them forever.

Pot had grown. His belly was huge and swollen with hot, red seed. It was the worst fire the men had ever seen. High flames of dark red, yellow, and orange pulled at them like the tongue of some evil, hungry beast.

Sin had never been so frightened.

He had spied on Pot since he was a small child, and this was beyond words. Beyond description. How was he going to explain to Cia?

Pot's belly grumbled and groaned; and searing, scalding ash spewed out. Sin had never seen such fury in the crater before.

"Tec!" Lef screamed above the noise of the volcano. "What are we going to do?"

The dome of molten rock and debris trembled and moaned like a woman giving birth. "We have got to get out of here." As they watched, the dome gave a loud moan, and fire billowed closer to their feet.

Sin grabbed Lef's arm, and turning, they began scrambling toward the valley floor. They ran, slipping and sliding. Every time one of them fell, the other helped him up. It seemed to take forever before they were on the valley floor, running as fast as a herd of frightened antelope toward the cave.

* * * *

They raced into the cave, yelling.
"It is not good! It is very bad!"
"We must leave, Cia!"
"Gather the children and as much as you can and run."
"Stop!"
Lef, Sin, and Cia were talking at once.

The panic in their voices was beginning to influence the rest of the clan, and if Cia didn't get control of the situation, she would have screaming women and crying babies to contend with, not to mention the men. They were already riled up because they could not leave without their leader's orders.

Cia put a firm hand on Sin's and Lef's arms. "Stop at once," she ordered in a quiet yet harsh voice.

The men's mouths slammed shut, and they gave each other guilty frowns.

"But—" Sin opened his mouth, and Cia put a hand over his lips.

"No!" She ordered. "The rest of you," she gestured toward the dwellers standing around wringing their hands, "Go about your business. I will call you when it is time to talk.

"Sin and Lef, sit down. Keep your mouths shut and act calm while Gem fixes your injuries. We will speak when she is done and not before."

Sin grumbled, and Cia tapped his lips with two fingers. "Do not speak."

Reluctantly, Sin and Lef sat down at Cia's home fire. Gem, the cave's medicine woman, brought her stone bowl of hot water and bag of herbs, and went about tending to the young men's cuts and scrapes.

Cia made herb tea while Gem worked. Neither woman spoke. Sin and Lef knew it was better to keep quiet until their leader wanted them to speak. An angry Cia was not a good thing.

Every time Sin shifted his bottom, Cia gave him a warning scowl. It was good to be the baby brother of the clan's leader, but she often treated him the same as everyone else. Long ago, she had told him she loved him, but even being her brother did not change the fact that she was the head of the clan and what she said was the final word.

Cia handed the men each a bowl of steaming tea and signed for them to drink.

Sin gagged but swallowed. "What is this, Cia? It tastes like dog poop smells."

"Just drink and do not ask questions. It will calm and sooth you."

When their tea bowls were empty, Gem was finished, and Cia thanked her for her help. Gem left them, and Cia spoke in a deadly quiet voice. "Tell me quickly and quietly what has happened to Pot. If you frighten the clan members, I will find some suitable punishment for you both, so be calm."

Lef looked at Sin. "You speak, brother."

"Pot's belly bulge has grown large and will soon burst. His flames are higher than any fire I have ever seen. It is fearsome, Cia. Very dangerous. Soon, he will boil over the top and explode. There is a large crack in Pot's side, and soon, his seed will flow from it. We must move the clan. Now!" Sin wanted to shout at his sister, but instead, he squeezed his hands together and prayed she would listen and believe.

"What side is this crack on?"

"Ours!"

"I hear you, my brother, but Gem is about to deliver, and we haven't found a safe cave."

"We do not have time to sit and wait. We must go now."

Cia frowned and began to pace. Her mate, the handsome, dark man, Let, who was Lef's adopted brother, followed her with his eyes and frowned also. "We have looked and looked and can't find a cave big enough for all of us, Sin."

"If Pot spills his guts, it will not matter. We will be burned alive, and I, for one, do not want to die." At least, not until he had taken Em to his bed and mated with her at least once.

"Do you want to die that way, my sister?"

"No, but..."

"Gather everything together. We must move." Sin decided to take matters into his own hands.

Let moved forward. "Come, Cia. We will move to the farthest valley from Pot and hope we can find shelter. At least it is the hot time and if we can't find caves, we will not freeze. Sin is right—we need to leave this place. Now!"

* * * *

It had been a struggle to get the dwellers out of the cave and moving, but somehow, they had managed. Cia and her mate led a straggling group of dwellers, numbering twenty-five, across the quivering valley at a pace that could only be described as slow.

Too slow.

Sin and Lef took up the rear, urging the women and children to hurry, but to no avail. The group had too many little ones and several pregnant women. They would never make it in time.

"Hurry," Sin urged one of the smaller children, and when the child didn't move fast enough, he picked him up and put him on his shoulders.

Lef also picked up a child and put her on his shoulders. The two young men began to trot and soon took over the lead. With their example and urging, the group picked up speed.

"Have you seen Em?" Sin asked Lef.

"Yes, she is with Ria. They are carrying Ria's sisters. Ria's father made a carrier of saplings and antelope skin, which he strapped to the girls' waists. They are dragging some of the household goods. The last time I looked back, they were at the end of the line."

Sin frowned and turned around to walk backward. "Yes, they are losing ground. I'm afraid they are tiring." He handed the small boy he was carrying on his shoulders to Lef and took off at a trot toward the back of the line.

"Stop," Sin told the young women when he reached them. He was furious when he saw each woman had a small child on her shoulders. It was understood in his society that the women did all the hard work, but angered him greatly when he noticed the women were both tied to an arm of a large sled. Tied like animals.

The women came to an abrupt halt when Sin yelled at them. It was unusual for the young men to speak to the young women without their fathers present. Sin smiled to ease their worry. "Untie the carrier from your waists, and I will drag it so you can move faster."

Em opened her mouth to protest, and Sin smiled and put his hand on her lips. They were trembling.

"Do not be afraid. I will watch over you, girl. You will be safe. I promise."

"But my father told us we must drag the sled and carry my little sisters. He will be angry if we do not obey," Ria said bravely.

Ria's father was known to have a violent temper and had been warned to control his anger or he would be put out of the clan. Cia's warning had only made Es angrier, but he no longer beat his family.

"He will not be angry," Sin assured her. "I will speak to him myself."

"We must go," Em insisted as the ground rose and heaved under their feet. Ash landed on her hair and she sneezed. Her hands, wrapped around her little sister's ankles, continued to tremble. "My father will also be very angry."

Sin gave her his most winning smile. "No. He will not." He put out a hand and began to loosen the antelope sinew strapping the carrier to her waist. Em put a gentle hand on his, and Sin's cock rustled, threatening to grow and show itself. How could her touch excite him now? There was no time for fucking. Pot was going to explode soon. Very soon.

"I will help you," Em said. Her gentle voice and soft hands caused his cock to rise and push its way out of his hunting pants. "Oh!" she gasped, spying his aroused penis.

Sin silently shoved his cock out of sight and continued to untangle the sinew holding the carrier. If he ignored the problem, it would go away.

Ria giggled, and Em hit her on the arm. "Silence," she ordered her friend, who immediately began to laugh out loud.

Sin's fingers refused to work. He couldn't seem to get the sinew to give way. He was about to lean forward and bite it when it loosened, and one side of the carrier was loose. He easily untangled the second sinew, wondering as he did why the touch of Ria's body under his fingers did nothing to him. In fact, his cock had drooped back where it belonged, snuggled against his balls.

It took a few moments to reattach the carrier to his lean waist, and with a sigh of relief, they were trotting to catch up with the rest of the dwellers. At the opening separating the valley from the next, the young women slipped through after helping Sin unstrap the carrier. Turning the carrier on its side, Sin dragged it through the narrow opening, and on the other side, reattached it to his waist.

Sin felt a lot better. They were away from the rumbling Pot. However, the earth continued to groan and heave, and ash drifted down on their heads. The whole group was beginning to look like a troop of elders. Sin feared they were still not safe in this valley. They would have to go much farther to avoid Pot's wrath.

The valley they had entered was a grassy plain intermittently broken by a tree or two. It was nowhere near as pleasant as the valley they'd been inhabiting for the past few years. There was some evidence of previous dwellers, but to Sin's eyes, the valley looked and felt empty. Sin had a feeling his sister and her mate had already been in this valley as they'd searched for a new cave for their group.

It was going to take days to cross this valley and get farther away from Pot's fury. Sin didn't think they had days. The way the ground moved under their feet, he thought they might only have one passing of Tec. They had to hurry.

When Sin was a child, Pot had exploded and sent debris and hot rocks spewing into the air, and boiling black rock had run down the side and filled a valley on the other side of where his group was dwelling. The clan had been very lucky. This time, they would not be so lucky, and Sin didn't want to wait around to find out if they would live or die by Pot's mighty hand.

To keep his mind off the death awaiting the group, Sin watched the movement of Em's firm bottom as she walked in front of him. He knew what she looked like naked. He and Lef had spent much time hiding in the bushes and rocks watching as she and Ria bathed. Oh, yes, he was very familiar with her body.

* * * *

Late in the day, the troop stopped and built a fire. As they walked, the men had spread out from the group and hunted, so there was fresh meat for the evening meal. Roasted rabbit and tubers made a filling meal. Some of the younger children had scouted and found water, so they drank their fill, and in the dawn's light, they would fill their water pouches for the day's trek ahead.

After a day of trembling and groaning, the ground seemed to settle, and all was silent. Pot was still spewing hot ash but was not as noisy as he had been for the past few days.

Later, there was much talk around the fire by the elders of the group. Speculation was high. They felt the troop was making a mistake and should not go by the findings of two young men.

Sin jumped at the accusation. "I am not a child," he protested. "I am a man. Soon, I will mate. I know what I saw, and I tell the truth. Pot is going to explode, and it will be soon. Pot may be sleeping tonight, but he will not sleep tomorrow."

Lef nodded in agreement, and Cia, coming to his defense, said, "Sin is not a child. Remember, we have been through this before. Last time, we were lucky. We are only being smart by moving. I, for one, do not want to die."

Two of the eldest of the troop spoke up in agreement. "We remember. You are right. We must get far away from Pot."

While Cia and the elders spoke, Sin moved silently around the fire until he was sitting near Em. He took a deep breath and was rewarded by her scent. It was hard to believe that with the air full of ash and smoke, he could still find her scent. Flowers and sun.

He slipped down behind her and could tell by the set of her slender shoulders that she was fully conscious of his presence. Squatting a few inches from her, he waited for her to say something. Like all the other young women of the troop, Em saved her words and laughter to share with her girl friends.

Sin waited patiently for her to speak, and when what seemed like a full day had passed and still no words came from her mouth, Sin whispered, "Are you frightened?"

Em shook her head and answered quietly. "Not yet."

The ground shifted and grumbled under their feet, and Em gasped as she fell back, landing on Sin.

"Oh. I am sorry, Sin." She jumped up and brushed off the back of her short skin skirt. "Now, I am beginning to be afraid. Pot is so unhappy."

Sin, who had spent the entire day thinking about Em's naked body, took advantage of her fear to wrap a firm arm around her and pull her close. "Don't be afraid. I will protect you the best I can."

At first Em's body was tight with obvious terror, but as the earth settled, she took advantage of his firm embrace and leaned against his chest. Together, they sank down to cuddle near the fire as many couples were doing. The night was dark and the noises strange. Nothing was as it had been in their familiar valley. Here, not only was Pot causing fear, but the night noises were louder and more terrifying.

The children gathered as much dry wood as they could find and piled it on the edge of the campsite. One of the men, Ket, added several pieces of the wood to the fire, and the flames leapt flickering bright and hot. Women gathered up the young children and settled them for the night while the men continued to discuss the following day's walk. Directions were argued and discarded.

Sin sat at the edge of the group, holding Em close to his chest. He couldn't get enough of the scent and feel of her slim body. She fit against him as if she was made just for him and his enjoyment. He watched and listened, hoping to learn what the final decision would be for tomorrow's travel.

The fire began to fade. The women, who had finally gotten the children to sleep, returned to find their mates. Nursing babies were fed one last time, and the troop began to split off into pairs. Bearskins were strewn about close to the fire for warmth and pleasure.

Em was limp against Sin's chest. She seemed to be dozing. Good. She had worked very hard all day and walked a long way. Tomorrow would be as long and hard.

Sin remained silent, watching Ket stirring the fire, adding small branches and banking it so there would be warmth much of the night. Ket had been chosen to be the night guard, and he would check the fire many times as was his duty. His friend Rio stopped to tell Ket he would join him later so he would not be alone.

Sin still felt the sting of rebuff. He and Lef had offered to do night watch, but the elders had ignored them. The young men thought it was because they had offended the elders when they had stepped in and said it was time to move.

The elders did not like to be questioned, but Sin knew with all his being that he was right and if they didn't keep moving they would all soon be dead. And, it would not be an easy death. They would be cooked alive.

* * * *

Em rested against Sin's large, muscular body. She had dreamed about this day since she had started bleeding in her ninth summer. She knew he watched her bathe. She and Ria went out of their way to make sure Sin and Lef were aware each time they went to the bathing pools.

Right now, Em wished she could bathe. It had been a hot, dirty day, and her hair was full of ash. Her body had slicked with sweat as they had walked through the valley. It had been a long, hard, fast trek; and she'd been exhausted by the time they had stopped under a grove of trees for the night.

The troop had been lucky to find the grove. The rest of this valley was mostly grass and rock.

The earth shook, and Em moved even closer to Sin. He wrapped his hard arms around her shoulders and buried his nose in her hair. "Don't," she whispered.

"Why?" he laughed lightly. "You smell like flowers."

"You lie. I smell like smoke and dirt." She pushed her hands against his chest, trying to put some space between their bodies.

"No," he protested, pulling her back against his chest. "I only smell flowers and woman."

She was too tired to argue, and Sin began humming a song. It was a song Lia had made up about love and laughter. Soon, her head was too heavy to hold up, and she rested, warm and safe, in Sin's arms.

* * * *

Em woke with a start when Sin's hand brushed across her breast, and her nipple peaked. Her belly rolled, and her cunt became wet.

"Sin? What are you doing? It feels very strange."

His soft laugh ticked her ear. "No man has touched you like this before have they little one?"

She shook her head.

"Good. I will be the one to make you happy. We will fuck. I will be careful and please you much."

Em nodded. The strange feelings had been with her since he touched her arms earlier when he removed the carrier she had been dragging behind her.

She had seen his cock poke its way out of his hunting pants, and she had almost put her hand on him. She and Ria had talked many times about the feel of a man's cock inside their bodies. Tonight, she was going to find out.

Sin's cock pushed against her hip. Feeling daring, Em slipped her hand between their bodies and touched the tip of his cock. Sin jolted, and his fingers tightened on her teat.

"Oh," Em sighed.

"Did I injure you?" Sin asked, pulling his hand away from her breast.

"No. Do it some more," she pleaded in a whisper. "I like it. It is nice." She moved her finger back and forth over the tip of his cock, and it became slick and wet. Did the slickness mean he was excited?

Sin's hips moved, and his cock grew under her fingers. "Am I hurting you?" Em asked, keeping her voice barely audible. More and more of the couples around the fire were locked in sexual embraces. Groans filled the air, and it was no longer Pot causing the disturbance.

Em and Sin were not innocent. Nudity and sexual activities were out in the open when living in a cave. Both had seen it all and more. It was not unusual for children to play at fucking, but it was frowned upon until women and men were in their eighteenth summers. This was the summer for Em and Sin to explore their sexuality.

Em let her finger wander down the length of Sin's large cock, and she was rewarded when the organ leapt and grew under her searching. Curious as to his width and breadth, she wrapped her hand around his cock. He was very big. Would he fit inside her? In truth, Em couldn't wait to find out.

"Will you fuck me?" she whispered, nuzzling her nose against his broad chest.

His hand cupped her breast, and with thumb and forefinger, he gently pinched her nipple. "What of your father?"

Em searched around the fire and found her father, Row, mounting Mar, his second mate. Em's mother had died when she was born, and Row had taken Mar to be his mate when Em was in her fourth summer.

"It would seem my father is very busy at the moment."

Sin laughed as he spotted Em's father. "Yes, I see."

Em nestled against Sin, baring both her breasts to his hands. "Touch me more," she demanded.

Sin immediately complied. Clasping her breasts in his rough hands, he ran his fingers back and forth across her nipples until they were swollen and stiff.

Em, not to be denied, was also busy teasing Sin's body. Turning so she was facing him, she put her legs over Sin, resting her thighs on his. Now, he had easy access to her breasts and open cunt, and she had a clear view of his rapidly growing cock. She loosened the flap at the front of his hunting pants, and his cock and balls were bare to her eyes and hands.

They were having a hard time sitting still. Sin's hips rose and fell at each stroke of her hands, and Em wiggled and sighed as Sin pinched and played with her nipples. "Suck me," she ordered. Sin frowned.

"What?" Em questioned. His furrowed brow made her wonder if she had done something wrong. Sin's frown turned back into a soft smile. "If I lean over you, you will not be able to touch my cock."

She grinned. "Oh, you like when I touch you?"

"Yes. Can't you feel my excitement?" He took her hand and moved it up and down his stiff shaft. "See how hard you make me."

He was wet and hot. "Yes. It is very nice. You are large. Almost as large as Lef's brother, Let."

"Oh, so you have been spying on Let?"

She giggled and smoothed more moisture over the head of his cock. "Well, yes. But he is mated and too old for me."

Sin's hips lifted to follow her hand. "I am not too old, and I want you for my mate."

She leaned forward and rubbed her nose on his before touching her lips to his. "I want to mate with you also."

"Lie down," Sin ordered, smoothing his hands down her body to clasp her waist.

"Not on the ground, Sin. We need a bearskin. This will be my first time, and I do not want to fuck on the rocks and dirt."

Sin slid his hands down the rest of her body and along her opened thighs. Slowly, he ran his hands over her thighs and up to her cunt. Using his thumbs, he opened her cunt and began stroking her clit. Em groaned and whimpered, lifting her hips off the ground. At first she had felt she was in charge, but now, with Sin's hands in her cunt, she lost control. All she wanted to do was let him put his cock into her body.

Moisture rolled out of her cunt and pooled on the ground under Em's hips. "More," she whimpered. "More."

"I would fuck you, Em."

"Yes. Yes."

Sin took his hands out of her cunt, and Em protested with a whimper.

"I will find us a bearskin." He lifted her legs and pushed her gently aside. "Take off your hunting skirt. I will be right back."

Sin stood, and his cock was at mouth level for Em. She could not resist and took him in her mouth before he could stop her. She had seen other women do this to their mates and had an idea what to do. Wrapping her tongue around his weeping cock, she sucked hard.

She clasped her hands around his hard ass and pulled him close. Sin's hips followed the motion of her sucking, and Em, oblivious to the people lounging around the camp fire, began to tug at Sin's hunting pants, trying to figure out how to get them off his hips.

Em couldn't believe she was sucking on Sin's handsome cock. She'd been thinking about it since she was a very young girl, and now, she was doing it. His cock was much larger than she had first realized, and she could not take him all the way into her mouth. She was very disappointed, but Sin didn't seem to notice. In fact if the motion of his hips told her anything, he was enjoying her sucking.

She was beside herself with desire. Her body trembled and shook from want. She whimpered and moaned around the cock stuffed in her mouth. Would he explode in her face?

She'd seen the other cave dwellers fuck many times before, and sucking a man until he exploded on a woman's face was quite common.

Nude, aroused men and women were often seen in the cave. When so many people lived in an enclosed space, there was little or no privacy. Em had been watching and learning since she was a small child. Nothing surprised her, and everything sexual excited her. She was ready to mate and make babies.

Her breasts swelled and ached for his touch. Her cunt ran with honey, and her whole body screamed for release.

The night was dark and full of strange noises and also familiar sounds. Other couples fucked and moaned while Pot, the volcano, continued to grumble and spew ash. The air was stifling hot, and yet the ground was cool and damp. The ash burned when it landed on bare skin.

Sin threw his head back and growled. "No, Em. No more. You must stop. I do not want to explode on your face. I want to be inside you." Clasping her head in his hands, he gently pulled his cock out of her mouth. When she protested, he touched his nose to hers and rubbed softly. "I will get a bearskin."

"Oh. Yes."

"Take off your skirt. I will return soon."

She was untying the sinews holding her skirt together when he strode away. He should not have left her. What if she changed her mind? But Em was right. They could not fuck the first time on the rocky ground. She deserved better. There had to be a spare bearskin around somewhere. Hopefully, it wouldn't take long to find a large, soft skin, and while he was gone, Em would not change her mind.

While he was searching, Sin thought about asking Em's father for his approval to mate with his daughter, but his cock was throbbing, and his balls ached for release. He didn't have time to wake her father, who had finished fucking Mar, and now lay asleep with a leg and arm thrown over his mate.

Better to fuck Em now and ask permission later.

* * * *

Em was having second and third thoughts. She shouldn't have let him walk away. She should have not insisted on the bearskin rug. So what if the ground was cold, rocky, and hard? It wouldn't have been the first time her butt had been rubbed on rocky ground.

Em sighed.

She really wanted her first time to be special, on a nice, soft skin. She wanted softness under her butt and Sin above her. She couldn't wait for him to slip his long, hard cock into her soft, wet cunt. She'd been thinking about this for a very long time, and if she was going to die in the burning rocks of the volcano, she wanted to die happy and satisfied.

Where was he? He should have been back by now.

Em, nude and nervous, began to pace in the space she'd found behind a boulder. No one could see her from their spots around the fire.

A hand grabbed her on the shoulder, and Em squealed, thinking it was her father. She turned and came face to face with her friend Ria. "What do you want, my sister? I thought you were sleeping."

Ria giggled, staring at Em's naked body. "I was, but Sin woke me looking for a bearskin. I had a feeling you were going to be fucking, and I wanted to come and see if it was true. Because you are naked, I guess you are going to fuck."

Em nodded and made no move to cover her nakedness. Why bother? Her friend had seen her naked many times.

"Have you asked your father if you could mate with Sin?"

Em shrugged her shoulders, and admitted she had not and didn't plan to. "Did Sin find a skin yet?"

"Not when I saw him."

"I hope he hurries."

Ria put a hand on Em's arm. "Are you afraid?"

Em squatted in the dirt and stared into the dark. "Yes. Aren't you?" She knew Ria had not fucked anyone yet either and was dying to be taken by Lef, but he was a shy man. Quiet and always shadowing Sin. Ria was getting tired of waiting for Lef to ask her father for her.

"A little."

"Why don't you go find Lef and rub noses with him for awhile? Let him touch your tits—it feels really nice. You will like it. Let him lick them and suck them."

"What will happen when my father finds out?"

"What can he do but give you to Lef as a mate? You want to be his mate, don't you?"

"Oh, yes."

"Then go to Lef. Rub against him, tease him, brush your tits against his bare back. Whatever it takes to get him to notice you. It will be worth it, I promise. If he will let you, be sure to play with his cock. It is like the softest cattail fluff on the outside, but the inside is as hard as a large rock. Just thinking about Sin's cock makes me wet."

Em peered around the edge of the boulder and did not see Sin. It was very dark. The air was full of ash and soot. The large fire built to keep away the night creatures was dying down to a low pile of red embers.

Sin was not going to return.

"Go to Lef, Ria. Open your legs for him. Let him lick you and suck your tits. It will be the most exciting thing you have ever done." *And it may be the last, if Pot has his way.*

Ria hugged Em and ran from behind the rocks in search of Lef. Em was sure Ria and Lef would be mates before the night was over. In the light of Tec, there would be two angry fathers, but with Pot about to explode, the fathers would be too busy moving their families and keeping the clan together to get into an argument with the young men.

Oh, Tec. What had she gotten herself into? What had she convinced Ria to do? They were going to be in so much trouble. She should call Ria back.

No.

Let her go. Let her enjoy what might be their last days in the valleys—their last days of life.

The ground rose and sank, as did Em's insides. How long did they have before Pot would explode? A deep grumble filled the air. Not long, it would seem.

Em couldn't stop pacing. Where was Sin? If he didn't return soon, Tec would begin climbing, and it would be light. They would not be able to fuck once it became light. Her father would see her and stop them.

Sinking to her haunches, knees spread, Em squatted and stared at Tec's sons. Their little fires gleamed so brightly.

A large, rough hand touched her shoulder. She knew it was Sin. His presence made the air around her buzz like the little flying beasts her mother called bees. She rubbed her cheek against his hand and purred.

His hands slid over her shoulders and cupped the fullness of her breasts, and Em could not stop the groan that ripped its way from her belly. "My mate," she crooned in a low voice.

"Yes, Em," Sin whispered in her ear.

His fingers were driving her mad. He touched each nipple so gently it was as if he'd brushed a flower across her skin. Crazy with hunger for his body, Em reached behind her and tried to touch his balls. He still stood, and she could not reach them from where she sat. He seemed to understand what she wanted and squatted behind her.

Sin hissed when her fingers closed over his swollen balls. "Did you find a bearskin, my mate?" Em asked in a low voice, gently rolling his balls through her fingers.

"Yes. I spread it over there." He motioned toward some large rocks. "We will be well hidden, and the ground is flat and dry. She continued to pet his balls, and Sin arched his back. "You make me feel so good. It is nice. We will play this game many times before Tec rises."

Afraid to turn and yet excited at what was to come, Em ran a finger up the length of Sin's over-large cock. There was no shame in nakedness. It was an accepted practice among the cave dwellers. It was especially nice during the heat of the dry months.

Em had seen Sin walk about without his work apron, and she knew every line of his beautiful body by heart.

Now, with her fingers, she was memorizing every inch of his cock and balls.

Sin groaned, and Em turned to place her free hand over his lips. "Silent, my mate, or we will be in trouble with my father."

Sin lost his balance, and they landed in a sprawl on the ground. Em giggled and nuzzled her nose against his neck. His special man-smell filled her nostrils, and her cunt began to weep. The scent and the feel of him were almost more than she could stand. She moved her body, trying to get closer to him, and succeeded in bumping his cock with her knee.

"Don't wiggle," Sin warned.

She stopped moving and lifted her head to gaze into his eyes. "Why? Is someone coming?"

Sin laughed silently, his belly lifting and lowering, and Em rode along with a smile. "No, my sweet mate, but your knee was a little too close to my man-shaft."

Em sucked in a deep breath. "Oh. I am sorry. I would not hurt you, Sin."

Sin put his large hands around her waist and lifted her easily and waited until she was standing before sitting up. "Go to the skin, Em, and lay down," he directed. "We will fuck now."

Em put a hand over her lips to hide the fact they were quivering. Suddenly, she was afraid. What if her father caught them? What if she did not like fucking? What if he hurt her?

Sin put a hand on her arm. "I would never hurt you, my mate. Never."

She bent and placed her hand under his firm chin. Leaning into him, she nuzzled his nose with hers and placed her lips against his. "Never?"

"Never," he assured her, returning her kiss. His sister and her mate had long ago learned to kiss and now, mates frequently kissed.

His kiss was wonderful—everything she had wanted and dreamed about. He seemed to be able to move her soul from her body with his lips. Em groaned and opened her lips to his tongue. His hands were again on her breasts, his fingers gently pinching her nipples while his tongue mimicked the act of fucking.

Em's knees weakened, and her heart leapt in her chest like a gazelle leaping over rocks. He must be able to feel her heart as it was rocking her whole body. His hands left her breasts to clasp her waist, pulling her body close. His hard, hot, large cock rubbed against her belly.

The heat of his aroused man-shaft burned its way through her body. Moisture trickled down the inside of her thigh.

"I want you now, my mate. Fuck me, Sin," she begged in a strangled voice she barely recognized.

Sin swept her up into his arms and clasped her close to his chest. "Yes. Now."

He laid her gently on the large animal skin he'd removed from the carrier he'd been pulling earlier in the day. He smiled when she raised her arms and swept her hair out from under her head. The action lifted and raised her beautiful breasts toward his hands.

She arched her back and spread her knees, letting Sin know she was ready for mating. He'd seen other girls use the exact same motion many times to welcome their mates, but still he waited. Fear made his hands sweat and his heart leap in his chest. Would he be man enough for her? Would it hurt the first time? Would her father kill him when he found out they had mated without his approval?

Too many worries crowded his head, making his ears hurt and his cock limp.

Em took a deep breath and held out her arms to Sin, and he forgot his fear. His cock rose to point toward the night sky. The hood of skin protecting the tip of his cock drew back, exposing the swollen, wet knob. He, too, was ready.

Sin knelt between her thighs and leaned forward. He nuzzled the tip of Em's breast, and she writhed and moaned so loudly, Sin feared someone would hear them. He placed a hand over her lips. "Silence," he ordered. "We must be silent, or your father will find us."

Em nodded, remaining quiet as he had directed.

Holding her breast with one hand, he suckled a nipple into his mouth and began stroking her soft belly with his other hand. Still silent, her strong legs supporting her, Em lifted her bottom off the skin. Her back arched, pushing against his fingers and mouth.

Eventually, he tangled his fingers in the fur guarding her woman's place. She whimpered when he ran his finger along the wet lips hiding her channel. Her legs sprawled open wider when he slid a finger into her moisture. He was surprised when her insides sucked at his finger the same way he sucked at her tit. What a strange sensation.

Sin was becoming anxious to slide his cock into her body. Was it too soon? He'd seen other men greet their mates with nose nuzzles and immediately mount them. Something told him Em deserved better than a quick greeting fuck.

Even though Em was young, she seemed to know what to do to please a man. Her hands were everywhere on his body, and the touch of her fingers was driving Sin crazy. His cock thumped against her thigh, and Em opened her legs wider.

"Put it in," Em whimpered.

"Wait," Sin pleaded. "I want to lick you. I want to taste your honey."

"Hurry," she groaned, digging her fingers into his hair to direct him to her woman's place. "Hurry, hurry, hurry…"

"No. I will not hurry. I will taste you and drink of you and make you happy."

Her body swayed as she arched her hips higher off the fur rug.

Sin bent close and inhaled her scent. She smelled of woman. Hot, welcoming woman.

Under their bodies, the earth heaved and groaned as though it, too, were making love.

Em opened her mouth to cry out, and Sin put his finger over her lips. "Quiet."

"I can't wait, Sin. Hurry," she whispered.

He parted the lips of her sex gently and dipped into her essence. Putting his finger to his lips, he licked and was pleased. She tasted of wild honey. She was ready to be mated.

He leaned closer and put his lips on the hard bud of her clit, and Em whimpered.

"You like what I am doing?" Sin asked in a voice barely above the sound of the wind sighing through the trees.

"Ohhhh," Em answered.

He suckled her clit once again and waited for her body to stop twitching. She was close to exploding, and so was he. Sin could not wait a moment longer.

"I am going to put my cock inside you, Em. I might hurt you. If I do, I am sorry."

"I do not care. Hurry."

The earth heaved and groaned. Sin grasped his cock in both hands and slowly entered her open body. Em's groan matched the earth's noises. Her hips lifted off the ground, and her body pulled him in. There was no stopping. He would not be able to stop even if Em's father grabbed him by the neck and flung him aside.

Her internal barrier was strong, and it took several moments of hard work to break through. Em did not fight him but continued to urge Sin on with whimpers. "Hurry, hurry, hurry…"

A great cacophony of sounds came from the volcano, and at the same moment, Sin and Em reached their own explosions.

Under their bodies, the earth rose and dropped, and if Sin hadn't been so entrenched in Em, he would have fallen away from her.

Like them, the earth continued to shudder and shake for many minutes, and Sin wasn't sure if it was because he had taken Em or if it was the volcano.

The earth dropped sickeningly, and Sin shuddered as the last of his hot seed flew into Em. With a sigh, Sin collapsed on her breast and lay as if dead.

"Thank you, Sin," Em whispered in his ear.

"It was good?"

"Oh, yes. It was very good."

"I am glad. I tried hard to make it last, but your woman's place…"

"My cunt?" Em reminded him of the words he had learned growing up. Since his sister Cia had started her own clan she had taught them many, many words. Some for making love, some for daily living, and some for fun.

Tonight was for loving and fun.

"Yes, your cunt held me so tightly I could not stop the explosion."

Em sighed. "I think Pot is going to explode also."

Sin nodded and suckled at Em's nipple. "I am afraid Pot exploded while we were fucking."

"Oh? I thought the earth moved because of you."

He chuckled. "It was because of me *and* Pot."

The night passed too rapidly for the two new lovers, but for some of the other dwellers, it was a frightening night. Pot continued to spew and groan and rumble its warnings of imminent danger. Pot exploded at least four times in the night, and so, also, did Sin.

Pot's explosions were small compared to the explosions Sin experienced.

Not long before the rising of Tec, Sin left Em and crawled into his sleeping rug. It wasn't many moments before his eyes closed and he fell deeply asleep.

Lef had to kick Sin awake, which left Sin angry and aching. He was grumbling while he loaded the carrier for the girls, and Em stood silently to the side.

Em seemed terrified. Sin wasn't sure if it was because of him or if the noise Pot continued to make frightened her.

"Do not fear," Sin said. "We will be out of this valley before Pot explodes again."

"Are you sure?" Ria asked, walking up to the group.

Lef put a hand on Ria's shoulder. "We are going to be safe. I promise you."

The air was scalding hot and full of soot and ashes, making it hard to breath. The old people were coughing and wheezing. The younger people were beginning to cough and wheeze also.

Sin searched through all the things stacked on the carrier and found a large piece of tanned skin so thin he could almost see through it. He took his flint rock, cut it into pieces, and carefully punched two holes in each piece. Also among the things on the carrier, he found pieces of sinew, and he made as many mouth and nose coverings as he could for the dwellers. It took precious time, but with Em, Lef, and Ria's help, it went quickly, and soon, the dwellers were trooping across the valley, away from Pot and his horrible fire.

* * * *

The passing of Tec seemed slow to Em, who was pulling the carrier with Ria's help. Today, they were getting farther and farther behind the dwellers as they walked across the grass-filled valley.

Em was frightened. Pot had been blowing hot ash all morning, and the air was full of stinging grit. Would they ever get to the opening to the next valley?

"We are too slow, sister," Ria said, her voice full of fear.

"I know, but the carrier is heavy, and I am so tired."

"I am also. We should not have spent the night fucking, I guess," Ria admitted.

"Does your father know?"

"No, does yours?"

Em shook her head. "No, and I am not going to tell him. If Sin wants me, he will have to ask my father. I am going to be silent."

"I am waiting for Lef to ask for me also. Maybe we should not have mated with them," Ria said, shaking her head.

"Oh, but Ria, it was so good."

Ria laughed behind her mask. "Oh, yes. It was good."

"Do you want to do it again?"

"Yes, and soon."

The young women laughed.

"Where is Sin?"

"I do not know. I haven't seen him since he made the masks and walked away with Lef."

The women stopped, and Ria wiped her forehead. "I am so hot."

Pot rumbled and shook the valley, and the two women grabbed the carrier and took off again at a steady pace.

Sin and Lef had wandered far afield from the troop as they hunted for fresh meat for their evening meal. The dwellers were too frightened to stop for a midday meal, instead opting to gnaw on dried fish and salted meat as they walked.

Sin and Lef sat on a high rock, nibbling on dried fish and berries. Far ahead of them and off to the side of the valley, the straggling line of the troop could be seen.

"We have not seen one animal this day," Lef said, shaking his head.

Sin sighed and nibbled on more berries. "No. I think they are all gone because of Pot. They are as afraid as the rest of us."

"Do we have time to fish? I saw many fish in the river."

Hot ash landed on Sin's shoulders, and he brushed it away before it could burn him. "We must hurry, my brother, because I fear Pot is about to explode."

Lef jumped off the rock. "There is a shallow pool down in the gully over there," he said, pointing. "I have my spear, and you have yours. Let us hurry. I want to catch up with the troop. I fear for Ria's safety."

"I worry also for Em's life. I am afraid if we do not get into the next valley, we will all be dead soon, and I don't know about you, but I am too young to die. I still have more fucking to do. I want to make Em my mate and have children. I want to live to be old."

Sin jumped down next to his friend, and they trotted toward the pool Lef had found. There, they stood silently watching the fish for a moment. Lef was right—there were many fish, and the pool was shallow. Heat had probably made some of the water disappear, and the fish were swimming around in slow circles.

Long ago, the dwellers had discovered water disappeared when it boiled or was hot for a long time.

The water in the pool was warm enough to put the fish to sleep. "It will be easy to spear many fish," Sin said immediately, aiming for and spearing a large fish. Soon, they had more than enough fish for the evening meal and some to dry.

The men rigged up a carrier and strapped down the fish with sinew. Balancing the carrier between them, they made their way quickly across the valley and soon met up with the dwellers.

"Do you see Em and Ria?" Sin asked Lef.

"No, I do not see them."

"I am afraid they have been left behind yet again. Does her father care so little for her?"

Lef shrugged his shoulders. "She is a woman. Row wanted sons, and he has only daughters. I do not think he will care if something happens to her."

"He is a harsh man. I do not want her hurt because I *do* care." Sin's anger simmered like a boiling bowl of water. Row needed to be strung up for the animals to feast on. There was no time for retaliation, but soon, Sin would have it out with Row. Em was a priceless gem to be worshiped and adored, not discarded on the side of the road.

Sin handed the carrier of fish to two of the younger dwellers and turned to Lef. "I will go to find the women. You try to get the troop to move faster. We do not have much time."

"Go to the head of the line," Sin continued. "Find my sister, Cia, and tell her we all must hurry. We have to get to the next valley before nightfall, or we will die."

Lef waved and headed forward while Sin, moving like the wind, ran through the grasses searching for Em. His beautiful Em and Lef's Ria.

Where are they?

Sin was not going to panic. Panic would do no good and would be a waste of time. He had to find the women and get them moved to safety.

It was only by luck that Sin found Ria and Em. The grass was higher than their heads, and both women were sitting on the ground crying.

The only reason he found them was because the wind carried their sobs to his ears.

Squatting beside Em, Sin put a hand on her shaking shoulder. "What has happened, little one?"

"We are lost and tired," she sobbed. "Ria fell down, and now, her foot hurts."

Sin turned to Ria and picked up her foot. It was bleeding from a large, deep cut. "I will carry you, Ria. Can you lift the carrier by yourself, Em?"

"I think so, but I can't pull it alone."

"I know, but I can," Sin assured her. "Climb onto my shoulders," he told Ria. He waited patiently for her to get situated. "Now, wrap your legs around my neck and hold on to my head."

He grinned behind his mask. Lef was going to be angry when he saw Ria riding on his shoulders, but he had to get them moving fast. He was strong and could run with Ria on his shoulders. He hoped Em was strong enough to keep up with them.

"Em, pick up the carrier and put the handles in my hands." Sin put his hands behind him, waiting patiently. Em followed his directions, and soon, the handles of the carrier rested in his palms. With Em at his side and Ria hanging on for dear life, he took off at a steady trot.

If they got out of this valley alive, Em was going to be a perfect mate. She did as he told her, and she was now keeping up with Sin as he ran to find the dwellers.

The carrier bumped along behind him, and Sin was more than once tempted to leave it lying on the ground and let Row worry about his missing goods when they set up dwellings in the next valley. It was Row's fault the two women had gotten lost, and it was Row's fault they were all going to die if they didn't hurry up and get to the other valley.

Sin was not in the mood to die this day.

Em, sensing his anger, put a hand on his aching arm. "I know you will save us, Sin. You are very strong and brave."

Her tender touch gave him the strength to continue running, even though the air was scalding and he could barely breathe. "It is for you I am brave, little one."

"I love you," she said, keeping up with him.

"And I you," he answered. "You are very brave, Em. Are you tired? Do you want to rest?" She'd been running alongside him for miles in the heat. She had to be exhausted.

"No, for you, I will be strong. I can keep going, Sin."

* * * *

It was impossible to tell if it was night or day. The dust and smoke were too thick to see Tec. The dwellers struggled to the third valley and collapsed on the other side of the mountain wall.

"Come," Sin demanded of the younger men. "We must fill the opening in the wall with rocks and dirt."

"What good will it do?" Lef groused. "Besides, I am too tired to move."

"It may be the only thing protecting us from Pot's anger. The firewater pouring from his top will burn everything in its path. I am hoping we can stop it before it gets to this valley."

"I will help." Em stood and moved to join Sin and Lef.

"I will also." Ria joined the group.

Others stood and stumbled to the wall. It seemed to take forever, but eventually, they had the fissure in the mountain wall closed as tightly as they could. They lost count of how many rocks, large and small, had been jammed into the opening.

Cia, Sin's sister and the leader of the clan, supervised from a large boulder. Her mate, Let, carried the rocks to the younger men, who jammed them in place, and the women plastered it all with a mud mixture they made of dirt, dry grass, and water from a small pond they had found.

Standing back, Sin sighed. It would have to do. There was no more time.

Cia must have agreed, because she stood on her boulder and pointed up the side of the valley. "We will go up from here. There are many caves." The air was still full of so much hot soot it was hard to see their leader.

"You and you," Cia pointed to Sin and Lef, "and you, my mate." She pointed to Let. "Take some of the younger men and run through the valley. Find out if there are any other dwellers here and if there is enough food for us all. If not, we will have to move on in a day or two. But first, we must rest. It has been a hard two passings of Tec, and we are all tired."

Sin's heart sank. He wanted to stay with Em. It had been a hard trek, and he ached to hold her body in his arms. More than anything, he wanted to lie with her next to him all night. He wanted to fuck her until she was limp as a willow branch.

Part of the troop followed Cia to the hills and open caves, and a few young men followed Let, Lef, and Sin as they headed across the valley floor in search of food and dwellers.

Let's legs were long and strong, and soon, he was far ahead of the younger men. Sin and Lef planned to split off, taking two men apiece, and go in separate directions. If they spread out, they would be able to search the valley faster.

Sin poked his friend in the side. "Did you fuck Ria?"

Lef's eyes crinkled, and he chuckled. "I will not tell."

Sin hit Lef on the arm. "Tell me, Lef."

Lef's grin grew so big it stretched his mask. "Yes. And you, Sin. Did you fuck Em?"

Sin nodded.

"Was it good, my brother?"

Behind his mask, Sin also smiled and chuckled. "Oh, yes. She was so hot and tight inside."

"So was Ria. I thought she had burned my cock. But it is still there, and every time I'm around Ria, my cock grows."

Sin sighed. "I have been afraid all this day, but whenever I think of Em, my cock becomes strong and brave. I can't wait to have her again. I hope it will be tonight."

"Will you have to pay her father for her?"

"I have nothing since we left the old valley in such a hurry. What can I offer, except myself?"

"Mmm, perhaps we will find something worth killing here in this valley and you won't have to plead for her to be your mate."

Pleading was demeaning. Most young dwellers would rather die than plead for any woman's hand. Em was not any woman. She was Em, and she was worth more than any other woman in the clan. Sin wanted Em for his mate so much he was willing to plead, beg, whatever it took to have her for a mate.

Eventually, the two men split off, each taking three of the younger men. They all searched until it was almost too dark to see. They found no more dwellers, but there seemed to be plenty of animals to eat. There was even a grassy plain for grazing the few tamed animals the group kept. There was also a level place for the women to plant the fruit trees, berry vines, and maize plants they had rescued from their previous home.

There were a small river and several streams leading off the river, and all seemed to be teeming with fish. There was a forest thick with trees of all kinds. Some even bore hard fruit, which popped open when hit with a rock. The insides looked safe to eat. Someone brave would have to try it first.

Sin sent Kem, one of the young boys, to gather as many of the hard fruits as he could. He'd let the women decide what to do with them.

If Pot didn't ruin their new home, Sin knew in his heart this would be a great place to dwell.

The valley was cool and pleasant, with a slight breeze and no soot or smoke. They had come a very long way from their old caves.

* * * *

The men camped out in the middle of the valley for the night. They made fires, and cooked fish and roots to ease their hunger pangs. Sin stood on a tall rock and could see Let's fire and Lef's fire and knew they were all camped for the night.

The night was full of strange sounds—animals none of the dwellers had heard before seemed to be moving about. None came close, possibly deterred by the light of the fires.

Sin lay on his bearskin rug, arms crossed behind his head, thinking about his night in Em's arms and in her body. He could still feel her cunt, hot and wet, wrapped around his cock.

He slipped his hand down his body to clasp his cock in his hand. With slow strokes, he pushed back the skin protecting the end of his shaft and wished the hands on his cock were Em's. They weren't, but he would have to make do with his own hands. It wasn't unusual for a man to relieve himself when on a hunting expedition. No one would care if a slight groan issued from his lips when he exploded his seed.

Thinking of Em made it easy to quickly reach satisfaction. A loud moan left Sin's lips as he shot his seed into the air.

Someone cleared his throat, and Sin sighed and turned to find Lem, who was a few years older than he, kneeling next to Sin's bed.

"Are you lonely, my friend?" Lem whispered. Lem was a man with words and did not use his hands to converse unless it was with the old ones.

Sin nodded. "I miss my mate."

"Mmm, you have a mate?"

"Yes, but you must not tell her father, because I haven't asked for her hand yet."

"Oh? Who is it?"

"It is Em," Sin admitted in a whisper.

Lem leaned close to Sin. "I will be silent, Sin. I see you are still aching for her body. I can ease your hunger, my friend."

"You would help me, Lem?"

Lem and Sin spoke in low whispers while the others around them slept. Pit, the night guard, had his back to the camp and seemed to be staring off into the night. Sin had a feeling Pit was sleeping, but since Pit was sitting straight, no one could tell from where they lay. It didn't matter—the moment Pit heard one leaf crackle, he would be on his feet, spear at the ready.

"Well," Lem whispered.

Sin realized Lem's cock was standing straight up and the tip was moist. "You are very large, Lem. You will not hurt me?"

Lem sighed and stroked a hand over his burgeoning cock, pushing the hood back as he did so. "No, my friend, I will be gentle."

Sin knew the mechanics of having sex with a male. He'd done it many times as a young boy with his friends, but they had been small at the time, and it had been fun. Lem was a grown man, and it would be far different.

Lem put his other hand on Sin's cock while he continued to stroke his own. "See how nice it feels."

Lem's hot breath tickled Sin's ear.

It did feel wonderful. Heat grew in Sin's balls, and his back arched. Moisture formed on the tip of his cock, and Lem used the juice to wet Sin's cock so his hands would slide up and down the shaft easier.

"See, my friend, it does not hurt."

"No. Do it harder, Lem," Sin begged. He groaned when Lem's hand picked up speed. "I will come soon," Sin whimpered. "Harder."

Lem surprised Sin by flipping him onto his belly and lifting his ass in the air. Reaching under Sin's body, Lem continued to milk Sin's cock until pre-come wet his hand. "It is good?"

"Oh, yes," Sin groaned. "More…"

Lem took his wet hand and stroked it over Sin's anus. Sin clenched his butt cheeks and jerked away from Lem's searching finger. "What are you doing?"

"I am going to please you, my friend. Have you never done this before?"

"Yes, when I was young. The boys were much smaller than you. I want it to feel good, not hurt."

Lem laughed softly. "I will be careful. I know I am big. Let your ass cheeks loosen, and I will wet the way with my tongue."

Sin tried to relax his body, but it was not easy. He was frightened, yet excited beyond caring about the pain. His whole body jerked when Lem's long tongue invaded his ass. Lef, his dearest friend, had never done anything like this for Sin. It was very exciting. Sin's cock grew in length and width, growing so large and hard he ached.

Lem must have realized Sin's discomfort, because he reached under Sin's body and stroked his cock, milking it like the women of the tribe milked the goats they raised. His climax was very near, and Sin was relieved when Lem replaced his tongue with his cock. At first, Sin was tense, and Lem couldn't get the head of his cock past the puckered hole of Sin's anus. Lem was an expert at man-love, and within moments, he had Sin relaxed and open to his invasion.

"Yes," Sin groaned. "Go deeper."

Lem leaned over Sin's body and nuzzled his neck.

Sin arched and groaned. "Touch my cock."

Lem laughed softly in Sin's ear. "You like what I am doing?"

"Oh, Tec, yes. Hurry, Lem. I want to come. My balls hurt, and my cock aches for release."

Back and forth went Lem's hips, and his cock moved deeper and deeper into the depths of Sin's body.

Sin rocked back, urging Lem on with groans and moans.

Moments later, Sin's cock tightened, and his balls pulled hard against his body, and he shot his seed onto his bearskin rug. Soon, Lem shoved his cock deeper into Sin's tight ass, and Sin could feel Lem's hot seed flooding his insides. It was an amazing feeling. It was not as satisfying as making love with his mate, but it was a great way to relieve the hunger he had for Em.

Lem flopped down on Sin's skin rug, and Sin fell to his belly, exhausted. Turning to face Lem, Sin said, "Thank you, my friend. It was good. I feel happy."

Lem smiled so big Sin could see the sparkle of his teeth in the light of the fire. "I am glad." He put a rough hand on Sin's chin. "Will you help me?"

Sin stroked Lem's strong face. "Yes. Give me time to make more seed, and I will be on top. Will you like that, my friend?"

Lem grinned. "Yes. Very much." He cupped his hand over Sin's bottom. "You have a firm ass. I like it. You are good. It is hard to believe you have not done it since you were a child."

Sin's ass rose to meet the stroke of Lem's rough hand. "It is true. Keep on stroking me, and we will do it again soon, my friend."

"Good. I am ready," Lem assured Sin.

Sin could see Lem was not lying. His large cock pointed straight at the night sky, and the hood protecting his knob was rolled back, exposing the tip. Moisture formed and rolled down his shaft.

Sin put out a hand and stroked Lem's belly fur. "Nice. Soft," he told Lem. Next, Sin fingered Lem's man tits and was rewarded when Lem sucked in a deep breath and shivered. His cock dipped and swayed. "Yes. You are ready," Sin agreed, eager to make man-love again.

Sin rolled from his belly to his back, for he, too, was ready. "Kneel above me, Lem," Sin directed.

Lem did as told, and Sin urged his body forward so he could suck on Lem's cock. Lem's hips jerked back and forth, fucking Sin's mouth as Sin had fucked Em. "Now," Sin said, moving Lem's hips backward. "Lower your body until my cock is inside you." Lem gave him a strange look. "Do it. You will not be sorry, Lem."

Sin's cock was wet from his last explosion, and he slid into Lem's body with no trouble. Lifting his hips, he began to fuck Lem as if he were a woman. In and out. Higher and harder. At the same time, he tugged and stroked Lem's cock.

Within moments, both men shot their seed, Sin flooding Lem's body and Lem's seed wetting Sin's face.

It was most satisfying. Both men laughed quietly and rolled away from each other, wiping themselves on the bearskin.

"I am too tired, Lem, or I would do it again. You are good. I liked it. Did you?"

Lem was still laughing softly. "You are the best I have had in a long time. Thank you, Sin. If Em will not have you, I will. We would be most happy together."

"It was good, but Em is my soul mate. I will not need help once Em and I are mated."

Lem frowned. "I am here if you change your mind, my friend."

"I will not change my mind, Lem. I love Em and once we are mated I will not need to take my release from anyone but her.

"I am sorry you feel that way, Sin, for you are very pleasing to look at and to fuck." Lem stroked Sin's face gently.

Sin shook his head. "It will not happen again. You will have to find a new man or woman, and make them your mate for life. Then you will be happy also."

Lem shrugged and rolled over leaving Sin to face Lem's broad back.

"I am truly sorry my friend, but some things are not meant to be. I am counting on you to remain strong and to help us all find a safe home. Will you do that?"

"Yes." Lem's voice was a bare whisper on the wind. "Good night, Sin."

"Sleep well, my friend."

* * * *

The following morning found the tribe working hard to get ready for Pot to blow his top.

The tribe leaders were worried they hadn't traveled far enough, but this valley was so beautiful, the tribe didn't want to leave.

Pot, the volcano, continued to rumble and roar. Fire shot high in the air, and the valley became dark as night. Smoke billowed out like storm clouds gathering.

The elders sat in a modestly sized cave and argued their fate. Should they move? Should they stay? How far would Pot's black and red river flow if the side of Pot nearest this place opened? Could they run fast enough to avoid being burned alive?

The elders had no answers.

It was a very trying day as Pot grew louder and louder. The earth shook and heaved. The water in the small river running through the new valley was filled with soot. The women fussed and worried among themselves about the safety of the dirty water. Eventually, one of the younger women in the group figured out a way to strain the soot from the water. Her solution was easy, but it left many more problems to solve.

The men who had spent the night out in the wilderness returned with fresh meat and fish for the tribe. It didn't take the women long to have the meat cleaned, shoved onto sticks, and searing over fires. The little girls of the tribe dug roots and found berries to go with the meat, and soon, they were feasting.

Laughter echoed as the day continued to darken both because Tec had gone down behind the mountain and because Pot continued to spew billows of gray clouds and red fire.

The earth gave a great heave and shuddered. Children screamed and ran for their mothers' arms. Another tremendous heave, and a huge wall of rocks and dirt rose around the camp.

Mothers gathered their children, slung them under their arms, and grabbing all they could carry, began to make their way to the caves high above the valley floor. The men, too, gathered all they could carry and followed the women to the caves.

Sin searched the tribe for Em and her family. Em, too, seemed to be searching for him, because she held out a hand to him and cried his name. Her father grabbed her hand and began to drag her away.

"Stop!" Sin called loudly to be heard over the screams of the running women.

Em's father stopped, but when he saw who was calling to his daughter, he hit Em on the head with his closed fist and continued to pull her away.

Sin could not stand for a man to take his anger out on a woman, and he rushed forward, pushing running people out of his way as he went. "Give her to me, Row," he demanded when he reached Em and her father. "Now," he ordered.

Row wrapped his big hand in Em's long hair and yanked her to the ground. On her knees, Em trembled, and tears ran down her face, leaving a track in the soot. "She is mine, and she will do as I say." Row's face was as dark as the stones of the mountain. He yanked at her hair to prove she was his to do with as he pleased.

Anger filled Sin's chest. If Row did not stop hurting Em, Sin would kill him. It seemed the only way to stop the man from injuring Em further.

Em's eyes were glazed and vacant. The last blow to her head seemed to have knocked her senseless.

Sin felt no fear of Row, only murderous rage at his treatment of Em. He flexed his arms to show how strong he was. He was larger and more muscular than Row. "She is mine, Row. We have mated."

At his words, Row's face turned black with rage. He drug Em up by her hair and struck her with his closed fist.

"No. Do not hit her again. She is mine. Give her to me, Row."

Row threw Em to the side and put both his hands out to shove Sin aside. Sin laughed and shoved back with all his might. Row landed on his ass in the dirt. The hate in Row's eyes finally brought fear to Sin. Was Row going to kill Em to get even with him for their mating?

Sin picked up the angry Row and lifted him high in the air before throwing him to the ground. The air whooshed out of Row loudly, and Row lay back, silent and spent.

Sin, breathless with rage, rested his hands on his knees, gathering strength for the next round, but Row surprised him by crawling to his knees before standing up and turning his back on Sin.

Sin clenched his fists, ready for battle in case Row turned on him, but instead, Row walked to his daughter and kicked Em in the side.

Em screamed, and Sin rushed to her.

Row ignored the scream, picked up his belongings, and began to walk away. "Take her, then. She is worthless to me now." Row growled and stalked away.

Sin lifted Em gently and cradled her close to his chest. "I am sorry, Em. I wanted to save you from his anger. I should not have told him the truth. It only served to anger him more, and now, he has hurt you."

Em's tears slowed, and her breathing eased. She nuzzled against Sin's neck. "My father has thrown me out. We have nowhere to go. What will we do, Sin? We need to get away from Pot."

"I have found a place for us. It is big enough for us, and Ria and Lef. We will be fine. Lef has been working on cleaning and readying the cave for us. Hold on to me, and I will carry you there."

* * * *

"You have done well, my friend," Sin told Lef after he had settled Em on one of the bearskin beds.

"I'm glad you are pleased. I hope it is warm enough in here. I hurried to build a fire. It was cold and damp." He looked at the still-whimpering Em. "I did not know you would have Em with you this night. What happened? How did you pay her father?"

Sin frowned. "I had to fight her father for her. He was beating her, and I could not let him hurt her."

"Ah." Lef understood. "You told him you had mated with Em?"

"Yes."

"Her father must have been very angry with you."

"He seemed angrier with Em, but she is smaller, and he was able to hurt her easily. He kept hitting her in the head with his fist. I told him to stop, and he would not. I could not stand it any longer. I picked him up and threw him to the ground. I thought he would fight me, but instead, he turned and kicked Em in the side." Sin clenched his fists. "If he had not left, I would have killed him. Row is a harsh man."

"Where is Ria?" Em asked, pushing herself into a sitting position.

Lef laughed. "Do not worry, little one. She is back in the scat cave. She will be here soon."

When Ria returned, she tended to her friend's wounds, and then she brewed bowls of the hot, brown liquid they all called *cof.* "I brought a large bag of beans with me, and two bean plants Em and I will plant when it is safe."

Sin nodded. "You are smart, Ria. Thank you."

Bleating echoed through the cave, and Ria laughed. "I also grabbed a goat for milk. Lef has stocked the cave with food and water. We will be fine for a while." She searched the men's eyes. "How long will we be here?"

Sin shrugged. "I do not know."

Lef frowned and shrugged also. "It could be days before Pot explodes. It could be tonight."

Lef sighed. "What was all the excitement about before you brought Em to our cave?"

Sin shivered. "The ground opened up, and a wall of dirt and rock surrounded the camp.

"The tribe began to scream, and the babies cried. Never in my life have I seen the ground open up and throw rocks from its bowels. We were all very frightened."

"I am sorry I missed it." Lef moved toward the opening of the cave to peer out. "I see what you mean. It is...I do not have words for what I see."

Ria, sitting next to Em, hugged her friend. "You must have been afraid, my sister."

Em shuddered. "It was awful until I saw Sin, and then I knew I would be safe."

Sin went to her side and kissed her gently. "From now on, Em, you are mine, and I will take care of you. You are my mate. My wife."

"I am?"

"Yes. You are my wife." Sin wrapped his arms around her trembling body and held her tightly.

Em smiled at her new husband. "You make me so very happy, my mate."

Later, during the night, the earth quaked and shook. Rocks and gravel fell around the four as they huddled under a skin rug. When the rumbling stopped for a few moments, Sin and Lef got up and went to stand in the cave doorway. It was nearly impossible to see anything due to the smoke hiding the moon. Every now and then, the moon would shimmer through for a moment, and the men were able to see that the valley had still survived.

Eventually, Sin and Lef curled their bodies around their women and drifted off to sleep.

* * * *

Tec climbed over the mountain and walked slowly across the sky, beaming shards of light into the cave. The heat of Tec woke Sin when it struck his face. He had been so tired when they had all bedded down for the night, and he could tell by the light on his face that it was later than usual. He should be up and hunting.

If Tec was giving off light, had Pot stopped?

Sin climbed silently out of the fur bed. Making his way to the cave opening, he checked the valley. There was a haze of gray on all the vegetation, but it was blessedly silent, and the ground no longer shook.

For the first time in days, Tec shone through the clouds of smoke, and Pot was silent. Was the volcano done blowing its top? Sin tapped his chest with a closed fist for luck.

Silent as a cave cat, Sin made his way to the scat cave.

He returned and squatted by the fire, stirring it to life. He watched his wife sleep while he dipped water into a large bowl. He added ground beans and let the cof come to a boil. He slid the large cof bowl to the side of the fire and left it to simmer slowly.

Sin knelt next to Em and whispered in her ear, "Wake, my love. I want to fuck you."

She stirred, and her eyes opened. A grin tipped the corners of her mouth. "I must visit the scat cave first, and then we will fuck. When you did not fuck me before we went to sleep, I thought it was because you no longer wanted me."

Sin brushed her hair out of her face. "I am sorry, Em. It had been a long trip, and I was very tired and my body hurt. You must know I will always love and want you. You are my mate for as long as we live. Pot will not take you from me. Row will not take you from me. You are mine, little one."

She pushed back the rabbit-skin blanket, showing him her pink-tipped titties. "I am not so little, Sin."

He ran his hand over her nipples and cupped her breasts. "No, you are not little. Hurry, Em. I want you."

She put a gentle hand on his rising shaft and gave a light squeeze. "I can see you are ready, my husband. I will hurry."

Sin, unashamed, watched Lef wake and begin rubbing his hands over Ria's small breasts. He wished Em would hurry, because Lef's actions were making him hard and full. His balls ached. He wanted to be inside of his mate. He needed to feel her heat and the tightness of her cunt surrounding his cock.

Ria noticed Sin staring and smiled. "You should not be watching us, Sin. Where is Em?"

Lef turned his head and frowned. "Yes, my friend, where is your wife? Your shaft is large and weeping."

Sin fingered the tip of his cock. "I know it is, my brother. She is in the scat cave. Go back to what you were doing. Do not worry about us. We will be busy soon. I will stop watching."

Ria opened her mouth, and Lef put three fingers over her lips. "Silence, woman. I am busy here, and I need you to help me."

Ria rubbed her hand on Lef's chest. "I am here for you, my husband. Put your finger in my pussy, and you will see how wet I am for you."

Sin lay back on the bearskin bedding. He put his hands behind his head and waited impatiently for Em to return. He was about to go find her when Em strolled back to their bed. Her large breasts swayed, and Sin's cock grew bigger.

"Touch me, woman. I want your mouth on me."

Em turned to see what Lef and Ria were doing and quickly turned back to her husband. "They are fucking," she whispered.

"Yes, they are. We will be also, as soon as you come closer." Sin wiggled his eyebrows and grinned at his beautiful, naked wife. "Do not watch them. They are busy."

"Will they care if we fuck?" Em whispered, kneeling beside her husband.

"I do not think so. They are playing and having too much fun to notice what we are doing. What does it matter? You have seen others fuck when we all lived together in the old cave."

She giggled and clasped her hands around his shaft. "You are right. No one will care." She leaned forward and licked the tip of his cock. Another bead of moisture formed, and Em licked it off.

Sin's hips lifted off the skins, and he groaned when Em licked him for the third time. Her tongue was hot and exciting. Her small hands moved slowly up and down. His cock was growing longer and fuller by the moment. His balls were also full and aching. He was going to blow like Pot. Soon.

When Em was busy sucking his cock, Sin put a hand on her pussy and slid a finger inside of her. She was wet and ready. Her hips jerked with each movement of his finger, and her honey ran down his hand.

Sin finger-fucked her until she was moaning loudly. Her mouth was full of cock, so the sound came out more as a groan.

Sin couldn't wait any longer. He pried his cock out of her sucking mouth, put his hands around her waist, and lifted Em until she was over him. She knew what to do instinctively and spread her legs, opening herself to his burgeoning shaft. She was so wet his large appendage easily slipped into her wet cunt, and her internal muscles clenched tightly around him.

Lef and Ria reached their climax just as Sin pushed high inside Em. The cries from their friends spurred Sin on. He clutched Em around the waist and lifted her and settled her back down again. Once, twice, three times, but his shaft grew and grew until his cock was too large, and she was so tight he couldn't move her without hurting her.

Sin licked a finger and reached between their bodies. He rubbed her clit slowly, and before long, moisture flowed from her body, and Sin was able to move inside her once again.

In and out Sin pushed. Up and down Em moved. His hips lifted off the fur bed, and she arched her back. A moan filled the cave, echoing off the rock walls.

"Ahhhh!"

"My wife! Now?" Sin growled. Em answered with a groan.

"Now?" Sin insisted.

"Yes, my husband. Now! Now! Now!"

They lay as one, gasping for breath. Em snuggled her head against Sin's shoulder, where it fit perfectly. Sin inhaled the scent of her and wanted her again and again. Em's body relaxed and Sin was sure she'd fallen asleep.

Sin was still hard and high inside Em when Lef laughed and said, "She is asleep, my friend. Lay her down and come have a bowl of cof. You have worn her out."

It wasn't easy to pull away from Em without waking her. But before long, Sin had Em settled on the fur bed, where he left her to sleep.

* * * *

Tec rose and fell many times, and Pot remained silent. The cave dwellers grew brave and began to plant crops for the cold season. Em and Ria planted their cof beans along with other roots and plants they had rescued from the old valley.

Em and Ria missed their woman's times and, giggling like girls, told their mates there would soon be two more joining their group. The men were too excited to say much. In fact, they ended up punching each other and laughing and tumbling around on the dirt floor like cave dogs.

All was perfect.

Sin could not believe his luck. He was mated to his perfect mate, living with his best friend and his mate. Now, he was going to be a father.

It would be a boy. There was no doubt.

Sin was confident his man-juice was so strong he would make only boys.

The other dwellers were also excited, for two babies meant their tribe was growing and healthy.

Nothing bad would happen to them now.

* * * *

Sin was sound asleep. He'd worked hard all day fishing, hunting, and cutting wood. Everything would be dried and stored for the cold season. The women had worked right alongside Sin and Lef. The women were especially tired now. Every day, their bellies grew larger and harder, filled with the little ones to come.

Sin's dreams were full of Em. Heavy with child, she was running across the valley toward him, screaming his name. Sin could see nothing, and yet she screamed and moaned. Was the child coming? No, it was too soon.

He could not reach her. She screamed his name over and over. Sin's legs would not move.

A river of hot, black water was between them.

Sin leaned over to touch the water and realized it was the boiling man-juice from Pot. The river of man-juice grew deeper and deeper, and Em screamed louder and louder.

Sin ran back and forth along the growing river, calling her name.

The world shook, and Sin continued to call Em.

"Sin. Wake up, my friend." Lef's voice broke into Sin's sleep.

"What?" Sin looked about the darkened cave, relieved to see only the glow of a banked fire and Em asleep against his body. Since she had become filled with his child, her body gave off more heat. No wonder he'd been dreaming about Pot and Pot's man-juice.

"Sin, are you awake?" Lef whispered, shaking Sin's arm.

Sin put his hand over Lef's. "Yes," he whispered. "What is wrong?"

"Pot has exploded. Didn't you hear it?"

"No. I was dreaming. Em was screaming, and Pot's man-juice was between us, and I couldn't reach her."

"Mmm, I heard you stirring and thought Pot had broken your sleep."

Sin pushed the skin rug off his body and sat up. "How bad is it?"

"Bad. Very bad."

Sin stood and walked to the cave opening. The sky was filled with scalding smoke and bits of boiling rock fragments. Pot had opened on the side facing their valley, and his hot man-juice boiled out at an amazing speed. Dark as night and red with fire, the boiling juice was moving rapidly toward their valley.

Lef was right—it was very bad. Where could they go? The volcano continued to rumble and groan, and more smoke and fire shot high in the air. As Sin watched, others ventured out of their sleeping caves and hurried to the valley floor. They were foolishly trying to save the fields when they should be running for their lives.

Sin ducked back inside and pulled Lef into a corner where the women could not hear them. "I think we must leave. Now."

"How? There is nowhere to go. We are dead."

"No. Take courage. I have been searching the cave, and there is another way out. It leads to a valley far from Pot."

Lef shook his friend. "Why have you not told me? I am your friend. Were you going to leave Ria and me here to die?"

Sin grasped Lef's trembling shoulders. "No. I would never leave without you and Ria, my brother-friend. How could I? We have been together since birth. What kind of man do you think I am?" Sin clenched his fist. "I should hit you for your stupid thoughts, but we don't have time for children's games."

Sin grabbed Lef's shoulders and held him until he stopped struggling. His body shook. Sin knew his friend well enough. Lef was no longer angry. He was frightened. Sin did not blame him for his fear. He, too, was frightened. "Lef? Listen to me."

Lef nodded. "I am frightened."

"I am also."

"What must I do?" Lef's voice showed his terror.

"We will wake the women, pack as much as we can carry, and each carry a fire stick. You will follow me."

Lef stared through the gloom at his mate. "I do not want to lose her, Sin. She is my heart."

Sin nodded. "I know what you say. Em is mine also. Now, wake your wife, and we will be off."

Heat from the river of fire filled their cave with smoke, soot and the glitter of colors brighter than Tec. It was becoming hard to breathe.

Lef woke his wife and she began to cough. Em joined her, coughing hard and Sin hoped they would not lose their babies with all the coughing.

Their coughing helped to cover some of the screams coming from the valley below. The few dwellers foolish enough to leave the safety of their caves were being burned to death.

At first, Em and Ria were too frightened to follow even the simplest of orders. They kept staring out of the cave and crying for the ones who were lost. Sin assured them he had seen many make it out of the valley before the black river had taken over the valley.

Eventually, with much urging and a lot of help from the men, they had the furs bundled and the food wrapped into manageable packets. Sin filled several gourds with water from the small waterfall that had started when the last blast of Pot had echoed through the valley. It was fortunate for them since otherwise there was no fresh water anywhere. The valley was now full of Pot's boiling black man-juice.

Sin corked the gourds with wads of grass. He gave them each a gourd, and then he helped strap the fur bundles on the women's backs. Lef strapped one on Sin, and Sin did the same for Lef.

Soon, they were ready to go.

Em and Ria moved to stare out of the cave opening.

"Do not look," Sin ordered.

"What of your sister, Cia and her mate Let? Are they going to be safe?"

"Little one you worry over much. Yes, they are safe. Let sent a runner yesterday saying they were many more valley's away and high in the mountains. The caves there are many and only the foolish didn't go with them."

Em wiped her eyes. "What of Gem and Og? Gem's child is only a few weeks old?"

"They also are safe with Cia and Let. Now, will you stop worrying and get ready to move to safety."

Em and Ria nodded, but were shaking all over and barely able to stand. They were so frightened. Sin put a firm arm around Em. "As we leave, grab a fire stick and hold it high. Do not be afraid. The fire will light our way. It is a long walk, but it will be worth the trip." He leaned over the fire and picked up a long, arm-thick branch. Following his example, Em picked up one as long but not as thick or heavy.

They waited while Lef and Ria picked out fire sticks. "Now, we are ready," Sin said firmly. "Follow me." He took Em's free hand and began walking toward the back of the cave.

"Wait," Em said, tugging Sin's hand. "Where are we going? We will die in here."

Sin put a firm arm around Em's body. "Be brave, little one. I know what I am doing." He gave her a kiss and grasped her hand in his. "Kiss your mate," he directed Lef. "We do not have much time."

It seemed as though they walked forever. The fire sticks held the dark at bay, and eventually, the two women stopped weeping, and with each step they took, they seemed to become stronger. What else could they do? If they stayed where they were, they would burn to death like the others.

Sin knew the way. When he'd found this tunnel, he'd never thought they would have to use it, and now, here they were escaping the man-juice of Pot by the skin of their teeth.

Em tugged at Sin's hand. "I am hungry, my mate. May we stop and eat? The child within is making me tired. I must rest."

Sin nodded and unstrapped his fur bundle, dropping it to the floor of yet another small cave. Sin had used his fingers to count the caves they had walked through, and this was the fourth cave. There were still three more caves to go before they would reach their goal.

Em and Ria found food and pieces of wood from their bundles and made a small fire to cook some cof. The fire also served to warm their feet and hands. The farther they had gone, the colder it had gotten.

"I am glad we wore our fur boots, Sin," Lef said, leaning over the fire to warm his hands. "It is very cold."

"I know, but it will get warmer when we are closer to the opening I found." He, too, warmed his hands. Both men were in the way, but the women did not complain. It would do no good. It was the cave dwellers' way—men's comfort and needs came first because without them, the tribe would die.

Ria handed out baked roots and dried meat, and Em filled small bowls with cof. All was silent, except for the sounds of chewing. No one wanted to ask what waited on the other side. Sin knew, but the others were afraid to question their new leader.

There was nothing left behind them. Would there be anything when the trip came to an end?

Em, who'd been leaning her back against the wall of the cave, fell asleep the moment she finished her meal. Sin watched her sleep and knew the women could not go on. It had been a hard struggle up and down sharp rocks and around water holes, all the time carrying heavy packs, fire sticks, and the babies in their bellies.

Where they sat was flat and dry. The small fire they'd built would continue to burn much of their sleep time. Sin had picked up pieces of black rock as they walked and put them in a skin sack he had hung over his shoulder. Now, he leaned forward and placed two large pieces of the coal in the small fire. It would keep them warm until it was time to walk again.

"Spread out the fur, Lef, and we will sleep."

Lef did as asked and pulled Ria down next to him on the fur rug. Sin lifted the limp Em and put her down next to Lef and Ria. He lay down next to Em and pulled another fur cover over them all. Em stirred and snuggled against Sin's body, seeking his heat. Before long, Sin's cock rose and began to rub against Em's skirt-covered bottom.

She moaned, and he pushed her skin skirt up. Now, they were flesh to flesh.

Her breathing had changed. She was awake. Sin put his arms around her and covered her firm breasts with his hands. She wiggled and squirmed, trying to get closer to him.

He rubbed his cock against her bottom crease, and she lifted her leg and draped it on his hip and leg, giving Sin easy access to her cunt. He pushed his cock back and forth between her cunt lips until he was slick with her honey, and then he slowly slid into her heat.

They barely moved or breathed. His fingers kneaded her nipples, and she sighed and shivered. His cock grew and grew until it was tightly embedded in her body, and his balls rubbed against her bottom.

In and out. Slowly, slowly. Hardly breathing, barely moving.

Sin nuzzled her neck and licked her soft, sweet skin, tasting her and teasing her, nipping and sucking her neck as he moved in and out of her sweetness.

Beside them, Ria and Lef were engaged in a much noisier sexual foray. Ria was a screamer, and Lef liked to hear her cry out his name.

The fur rug covering the two couples slipped down their bodies, leaving them exposed to the damp chill. No one seemed to notice. They were deep in the throes of earth-shaking climaxes.

Eventually, the lovers fell asleep under the blanket, curled together for warmth.

Since they had no Tec to judge time by, they slept until they were refreshed and well rested.

Before rising, the men made love to their wives once more. It was going to be a long walk, and they needed the comfort only their wives could offer them. Sexual prowess was empowering. The men needed to prove their male strength to each other and to their mates.

The women made a quick meal and boiled cof while the men talked of the trip ahead. Sin assured them it was not much farther. Perhaps by midday meal, they would be at the other side of the mountain they had been walking through.

The women cleared the site, and the men again prepared the backpacks, evenly distributing the weight amongst them. Sin was very proud of the women. They had promised to be strong and do what they could to help, and so far, they had exceeded his hopes. Both Em and Ria were brave women.

Sin put an arm around Em before putting her pack on her back. "I love you, my mate. Continue to be brave. We will be there soon. Is the child well? Is he still moving?"

Em put her arms around his waist and leaned sideways against his body, resting her head on his chest because her belly always got in the way. "The child is fine. He never stops moving. I am afraid once he is born, he will never sleep."

Sin laughed softly.

"It is a good sign, Sin. The child is strong."

"Like his brave mother." Sin kissed the top of her head.

Em sighed. "I love you, my mate. Because of you, I will be strong."

Sin kissed his mate with all the love he had in his heart. "We will find a good home soon, Em. Do not fear."

"I am not afraid."

"Good." Sin helped her into her backpack, and she helped him shrug on his. Tied firmly over their chests, the packs were secure and lighter since they had burned much of the wood they had all been carrying.

Lef lit the fire sticks in the small fire and handed them out.

"We are ready?" Sin smiled, and Em smiled back.

"I am ready. Lead us, my husband. I know you will lead us safely to the new place."

* * * *

Em tugged on Sin's arm. "I am so tired, Sin. Are we there?"

"Soon, Em." She was pale, and her lips were so tight together. Instead of being full and pouty, they were in a flat line of pain. "Sit, my mate, and we will rest for a short time." Sin removed the heavy pack from Em's back, and she lay down on the hard rock, using the fur-covered pack as a pillow.

Lef helped Ria out of her pack. "It has been a hard climb, my brother. Like Em, I'm beginning to wonder when we will be there. Are you sure we are going the right way?"

Sin grinned. "I am sure. I've been this way several times in the past few days while you all worked in the gardens."

"I wondered where you went when you disappeared." Lef laughed. "Now, we know."

"See the mark on the wall behind you, Lef?"

"Yes."

"That is my mark. We will be in the new valley very soon. Can't you feel how much warmer it is here? Haven't you seen it is lighter here?"

"I have noticed," Ria said quietly. "But I was afraid it was a dream. I am so tired."

"We can leave the packs here. This will make a good home for us." Sin squatted next to Em. "Can you walk a little farther without your pack?"

She nodded. "I can't wait to see the new valley."

"What if the valley is full of man-juice from Pot? What then, Sin?" Lef asked, for the first time putting into words everyone's fear.

"I do not know," Sin admitted. "We are young and strong. We will go on until we find another good valley."

Em wept silently. "I am so tired and afraid, Sin."

Sin wiped her face. "I know, my mate. I am afraid also, but we must go on."

Lef pulled the last few pieces of wood from his pack and started a fire. Sin dropped two black rocks into the blaze. "Lef and I will go and see what is on the outside. Stay here and rest. When we return, we will all make a meal."

Em and Ria began to cry. "Do not leave us."

Sin put an arm around Em. "There are no strange animals in this cave. I know, for I have checked it many times. Now, rest. Lef and I will be back soon."

Em lifted her face for Sin's kiss. "Be careful, Sin. I love you."

"We will return."

Em and Ria opened the fur packs and spread the bedding. Em picked one side of the cave, and Ria took the other. Next, Ria found the dried meat and vegetables while Em took a fire stick and a bowl and walked back into the cave. Earlier, the troop had walked past a clear pool of water.

In a short time, Em returned to the fire and poured some of the water into two separate cooking bowls—one for cof and one to cook the dried vegetables in. She pushed the cooking bowls close to the fire and squatted close to Ria on the bearskin rug she had rolled out.

Chores done, all the women could do was wait.

"What if they don't return?" Ria whispered.

Em put an arm around her friend. "I do not know."

"Can we go on without our husbands?"

Em shrugged. "I do not want to talk about it, Ria. They will come back."

* * * *

"Come with me, Em."

"Ah. You have returned." She smiled and held her hand out to him.

"You must see the new valley."

"Is it pretty?" Ria asked when Lef squatted next to her.

"The new valley is better than we ever imagined."

"Are there others?"

"Yes, many."

"They are different from us but seem friendly."

"Different how?" Em wondered.

Lef laughed. "They are dark, like my brother, Let."

"Ah."

The men pulled the women to their feet. "Come. See."

At the entrance to the cave, a wide ledge made it easy to look out over the valley spread before them.

Em searched for any sign of Pot. He could not be seen in this valley. The sky above was bright with the light of Tec. Below them, a small group of dark people gathered to watch them.

The women were dressed similarly to Em and Ria, in fur or tanned skin skirts. Some wore leather coverings over their breasts. Several had babies in their arms, and one tiny one tugged at his mother's nipple.

"They are pretty people," Em whispered. "They are smiling."

Sin laughed and raised a hand to the people waiting below. The men raised hands and signaled back. It seemed as if they were being welcomed to the valley.

Rough rocks make a stone stairway to the valley. The four picked their way carefully down to greet the strangers.

"Me, Weg," the man who seemed to be the leader said, stepping forward.

"I am Sin." He held his hand open, palm up.

Weg laid his open hand on Sin's. "Welcome, my brother."

Sin was pleased they spoke in words similar to theirs. "Thank you, my brother."

Sin put his arm out to Em and pulled her forward. "This is my mate, Em." Pointing, he continued, "This is my friend Lef and his mate, Ria."

Weg nodded. "Welcome. What brings you to our valley?"

The dark people behind Weg stepped closer to listen.

Sin looked up. These people were so tall, their skin dusky and smooth. They were a beautiful people. The men were heavily muscled from hard work, and the women were pretty, with large breasts and long legs. Even their babies were pretty.

"Our valley was filled with the boiling man-juice of Pot when he exploded. Our clan moved on as fast as we could. There were this many of us." He held up both hands to show his fingers. "We found a new valley, but the juice of Pot followed us, killing some. A few of our group moved on to a far away valley. We are the only ones left. I found a way through our cave to this valley."

Weg and his clan sighed, oh-ing and ah-ing at the story Sin told.

"We do not call the mountain Pot, but I know of what you speak. It was Rom who blows steam and smoke. He made noises, and the sky filled with dark heat. This many days." Weg held up one hand. "Rom filled the sky more than ever before. So Rom has blown up?"

Sin nodded. "It is so."

"If you wish, you may join us in this valley. We are different, yet we are the same. We welcome you."

Relief flooded Sin. "Thank you, my new brother. We are most happy to join your clan. May we live in the cave above?" Sin pointed up. "We are cave dwellers."

"Yes, the cave is yours." Weg pointed to his group. "We dwell on the ground in what we call huts."

Sin searched behind Weg and saw large round mounds of grasses and leaves. "Huts?"

"Yes. They are good in this valley. The light above, Sun, shines most of the time. It is always nice."

"Nice?"

"Yes, like this." Weg's hands gestured around the valley.

Sin couldn't believe their luck. The valley was perfect. The people were friendly, and from what Weg said, it was 'nice' all the time. What more could they ask for?

* * * *

Sin shook Em awake. "Come, my mate. It is time to sleep."

Em nodded silently.

Sin took her hand, picked up a fire stick, and wished their new family good sleep.

It was late. They had sat around a large fire speaking with their new family, gesturing when they ran out of words or couldn't understand each other's words. It had been a time to remember for as long as they had life.

Sin promised himself that when Tec arose the following day, he would record the story on the cave wall so they would never forget.

His troop followed him up the stone steps to their new home. The fire had gone out, so Em and Ria built it over again, and Sin added two black rocks. They would be warm for the night.

Em had picked out a small cave off of the large one for a scat cave. They all used the scat cave and then crawled into their fur beds.

* * * *

Tec crossed the sky above many times, and the moon followed, waxing and waning. The two groups became one family, working and hunting together.

One night, Sin sat on the ledge above the valley. He leaned against the rock wall, and Em rested against his chest. His cock and balls were heavy with seed. As always when Em was near, he wanted to fuck her.

He put his hands under her leather vest and cupped her breasts in his hands. Her breasts were large and firm, the nipples long and tense. She shivered, and Sin licked the curve of her neck. "I will fuck you, my mate."

She laughed and wiggled her bottom so his cock was squeezed between their bodies. "Yes. You always want to fuck, Sin. But first, I must tell you something."

He tweaked her nipples between his thumb and forefinger. "Tell me. I am listening."

"I do not think you are listening. You seem to be very busy with my tits."

"It feels nice. Yes?"

Her breasts seemed to grow even bigger and heavier. "Oh, yes, my mate. Do it some more. You play, and I will talk."

Sin's hand smoothed along her side and soon was curled around her female mound. One of his fingers slipped inside, and Em sighed.

"It is nice," Sin said, wiggling his finger. "You are so wet and sweet as honey."

She wiggled more, and his finger slipped in deeper. "Sin."

"Yes?"

"We will have a baby."

"We will?"

"Yes, my mate. We will."

"Are you sure it is not too soon? Tia is still a baby."

Em laughed. "Tia is running all the time now. She is busy with Ria and Lef's Dai along with the other small ones in the valley. Tia is no longer a baby."

"But how did that happen?"

"What?"

"Tia grows too fast. She is still a baby."

"No, Sin, she runs like the wind, and I can hardly keep up with her."

Sin shrugged his shoulders and sighed.

"It is time for another baby."

"Yes, you are right. When will we make this baby?"

Em laughed harder. "We already did, Sin. Are you blind?"

Sin frowned. "No."

"You have not noticed how large and heavy my breasts are?"

"Uh, yes. I like them very much. You have pretty tits."

She put her hands under her breasts and cradled them. "Thank you. Will you lick them now?"

"In a moment. We are having a baby?" Sin seemed perplexed.

Em waited patiently. Sin had to think on things. Would he be angry?

"It is good," he said. "Very good."

Em relaxed her body against his. She tipped her head back and twisted so he could kiss her.

"Em, I will fuck you now."

"Now?"

"Yes, turn around and lift your skirt," he ordered. "It will not hurt the child?"

"No. We fucked when Tia was inside, and it did not hurt her." She turned to face him. His cock was pointing toward the night sky.

She spit on her hands and rubbed his cock until moisture formed on the tip. She pushed back the hood protecting the tip of his cock and ran a finger over his slit.

Sin lifted his hips. "It is time, my mate. Let me into your wet heat."

Em, always a good mate, raised herself to her knees and opened her body to his cock. She looked deeply into his eyes and whispered, "Now, my husband?"

"Yes, now!" She was so wet. So hot. So welcoming. His cock fit perfectly into her cunt. It was tight as always. More of her moisture formed, and soon, he was sliding in and out of her body with ease.

Sin groaned, and his hips heaved. Em sank down, pulling his cock in deep. Sin pushed deeper still, and soon, they were exploding like Pot. Hot man-juice rolled down over Sin's balls and pooled under his butt.

Em moaned and cried out. Sin's whole body shuddered as he emptied himself into her.

It took a moment for Sin to recover his mind. "It was good? Did I hurt you, Em?"

Her laugh was as sweet as always, and Sin became hard again. "No, my mate. You are so strong and large. It was delicious."

"Delicious?"

"Yes, it is a new word Mai taught me. It means more than good. Like the sweetest fruit or the most tender meat. You are delicious."

He fucked her once again, careful this time to not go too deep. He did not want to hurt the baby.

Em snuggled in his arms, her head on his shoulder. Sin kissed her forehead. "You are my mate."

She nodded.

"This time, the child will be a boy?"

"I do not know, Sin. You love Tia. I do not think it will matter."

"You are right. It will not matter."

"I love you, Em."

"And, I love you, Sin."

"We will live here, and our children will grow here. Someday, they will make their own families. We will be safe and happy here for all time."

Em placed Sin's hand over her belly. "For all time."

THE END

WWW.CHERIEDENIS.NET

ABOUT THE AUTHOR

Cherie Denis realized she wanted to write when she started getting As on her English Lit. papers in 9th grade. Somehow, the writing got put to the side after she met her dream man as a senior in high school. The dream man and Cherie married when he was a sophomore in college and have been together ever since. They raised two daughters, a menagerie of pets including two guinea pigs (not recommended for small children) in Milwaukee, WI. The daughters got married and moved away leaving them empty nesters for several years before Cherie's mom moved in. After too many cold winters to count, Cherie, her beloved and mom moved to Nashville, TN where they are all happy as clams. Cherie is an active member of RWA and the local chapter Music City Romance Writers. Over the years, Cherie has held many jobs including running her own cake business, a doctor's receptionist, a dental assistant, a pharmacy clerk etc., etc. Cherie has been fascinated with erotica since she found where her dad hid his *Playboy* magazines when she was a girl. Her writing muse returned about seven years ago. With the encouragement of her prince and mom, she's been putting words to paper ever since and loving every minute of it.

Also by Cherie Denis

Siren Classic: *Cinnamon*

Also by Missy Lyons and Cherie Denis

Siren Classic: *Cowboys Don't Dance*
Ménage Amour: Twisted Sex Games: *Lynne's Love Triangle*

Available at
BOOKSTRAND.COM

Siren Publishing, Inc.
www.SirenPublishing.com